Alpha Rylan

Midika Crane

Inkitt

Prologue

"This really has become a trend now, hasn't it?"

The men stand in a tight semicircle in front of me, watching my every move with wary eyes. For whatever reason, they are trying to act as if their fingers don't quiver on their weapons, their feet ready to take a step backward if it came down to it.

Once upon a time, there were five men, however, I whittled it down to four. By accident, of course.

The commander in chief stands in the middle, the staff in his hand carved out of dark wood and sharpened at the tip with a metal cuff for holding at the base. Purity pack members are against using firearms, or even silver. Right now, though, I can see he wants to use such weapons on me and go against the alpha's rules.

"Get to your knees," he commands; the sternness in his voice wavering with every word.

My eyes roll unintentionally at the predictability of those four words. Commander Burke doesn't tend to bring any spice into our meetings-especially not lately. As the commander of an elite force created to protect the Purity pack itself, he probably would rather be doing anything else than this; *this* being chasing a girl aimlessly through the forest.

"And comply," we say at the same time, and he scowls. I, on the other hand, chuckle animatedly.

He casts a glance at the three men he brought with him. Did he see the scar on the one flanking his left's forehead? I surely did... I did when I inflicted it, too. It wouldn't have had to happen, had he not thrown himself at my feet without listening to my claims.

I hate it when they don't listen.

"What is this?" I muse, pulling my hand up, with my fingers out stretched. "The seventh time we have been through this?"

Commander Burke furrows a dark brow, which almost swallows his almond shaped eyes completely. He hated the talk. I do it every time though. It gets lonely sometimes, and, admittedly, a lot of my entertainment is found playing around with Alpha Rylan's guards.

"We wouldn't have to, if you would just give yourself in," Burke says irritably, his grip tightening around the handle of his weapon. Again, he's being predictable; has he been taught nothing? He does that when he's about to strike, like he might catch me off guard or something. When he notices my raised eyebrow, he will loosen it.

I sigh. "Have we not established that is not an option?"

The man on the edge of the group looks over to his commander. Why he comes along, I have no idea. Each and every time, without fail, he saunters up all confident, but runs the moment I decide to make my move. He's my favorite.

"Trust me, *creature*, we wouldn't be here if you weren't his mate," Burke says. Rylan won't tell them my real name, so they resorted to calling me 'creature'. I liked it too much to correct them.

If I wasn't Rylan's mate, a lot wouldn't happen.

I wouldn't be on the run. I wouldn't be poor. My family wouldn't have disowned me and my sister. I wouldn't live every moment wondering when his guards might burst through the undergrowth in a hunt for me. I have to give him credit for being so damn insistent... It's coming up to a year since we both found out. A year since I have been on the run.

I won't, *won't* live under his rules. I won't believe in the goddess. And neither will my sister.

"Nor would we have to, if you didn't steal...." Burke reminds me. My eyes narrow at him as he brings up a subject I'm done explaining to him. Stealing is a capital offense. So is murder. Only one of them I committed on purpose.

Again, he shouldn't have thrown himself at me. He practically forced my hand.

"You're right," I say blandly. "However, you're wasting your time chasing after someone who isn't your alpha's precious good girl."

It was at that moment that one of his guards struck. Actually, I had expected it around five minutes ago. The way he regarded me behind the cloth covering his mouth and nose gave me all the evidence I needed. Every now and again, he would jump slightly in anticipation, as if he were ready to commit, but changed his mind at the last minute.

I had already dislodged my weapon of choice from the tree against my trunk before he decided.

A heavy rock - one I found at the bottom of the local river-filled my palm, round and perfect for throwing. I prefer the long-ranged weapons; helps me sleep at night knowing I didn't get close enough to him to hurt him. I don't even have to look him in the eyes, as I launch the rock into the air, aiming directly between his eyes.

It hits him, instantly knocking the consciousness out of him. As he crumples to the floor, beside the rock, I'm quick to mask the flicker of guilt in my expression with anger. Anger I feel towards *him.*

A thick silence settles over us, until Burke cuts through it with a sigh. "A rock, that's new."

Usually I opt for a sharpened stick, like the ones they hold, however, not so long and extravagant. I tried a bone once too, however it didn't last without proper treatment. There's nothing that fancy out here in the forest. Burke doesn't listen when I tell him it's an unfair advantage.

This isn't a game to him, like it is to me. It's his job which is why I take great pleasure in putting it in jeopardy. Every time he drags injured men back to Rylan, I can imagine the possible consequences. Today is going to be no exception to the current streak we have going on.

"Honestly, I think you need better men," I comment, brushing my hands off on my thighs. My pants are tattered, but they do the job.

Burke rests the tip of his staff on the ground. "How about a bargain?"

My head perks up at the sound of that. Did he seriously just insinuate such a thing? Never, in the time Burke and I had met in the forest, has he ever offered me anything along the lines of a bargain. It was always the same old thing, so the sound of this has me a little excited.

"He wants to talk to you ... one last time," Burke tells me. "Then he will agree to letting you walk free."

My heart almost stops. Is he serious? Burke is an older man, which makes him twice as adamant as the young boys who usually stand by his side. This must be putting him through such mental torture, to know I may just get out free. The thought of that alone has me openly smiling with glee.

"Interesting," I say tersely. I can't decide if I should believe him. "What about?"

He shrugs; a very unusual motion for such a prestige. Even the two remaining boys look a little surprised. The blond one, who likes to run away, still looks uncomfortable though, and I feel the need to say 'boo' or something, to give him an excuse to flee. I would like one too, but I won't let them trace me back to my sister.

"You think I am allowed to know? You'll have to find out for yourself."

"Gross," I mutter, remembering every other conversation I've had with him. It's the same trash over and over again.

If I have to hear one word from that insufferable alpha one more time, I think I might rip my hair out. Of all the people in this world to not understand me, it's him. He seriously thinks keeping me locked within his pack walls constantly is going to turn me into a sweet darling. At least, that was his stance six months ago.

I haven't heard that voice since.

"You know what," I say, straightening my shoulders. "I'll talk to him. If he pulls anything, I'll kill him."

That much is true ... maybe. Every time I have been near him, I haven't felt the urge, but things have changed. I'm stronger now. Better.

I'm his personal fugitive. I'm planning to keep it that way.

Chapter One

This is dangerous. This is dangerous and stupid.

The reason why I decided to do this is primarily related to the lack of entertainment I get from the forest. Also, my incessant curiosity won't let me live this opportunity down.

My body strength from climbing trees all day allows me to heave my body weight onto the concrete structure, my feet coming under me, so I'm crouching. I won't make the mistake of standing up; the shadows will only conceal me so much.

Today, I've decided to take Commander Burke's delivered note from the alpha into consideration. Am I going to act on it past a certain point? Probably nota

Alpha Rylan promised that my sister and I would no longer be pursued by his guards, if I meet him one last time. This isn't something I actually believe, however, I'm interested in what he might have to say. It's been a year since I last saw him, and I want to know how he managed to keep his prized soldiers coming after *me*.

I've climbed this wall plenty of times. The concrete under my fingers is a familiar, rough feeling which I bask in for a moment. If this goes wrong, this might be the last time I do this.

You're here for a look, and a look only.

The purity pack stretches out in front of me, glittering lights and street noises invading my senses. This place is nothing like the forest that shrouds the outer walls, stopped only by the man-made structure meant to keep religion in, and sin out. Their alpha protects them well, from outlaws such as myself. He hates the fact that I can climb his precious wall and taint his precious people.

I step cautiously across the wide ridge. Rylan had cruel thick steel rods sharpened at the end installed to deter me from making it over, but it never has worked. I have no other choice. Food for my sister can only be found in this pack.

The alpha stated he would meet me by the wall at midnight, near the market place that wakes only at night. It's time has passed though; it's early morning at this point. Everyone would have gone home to wake up tomorrow at dawn for their daily events. They praise the moon only at midnight, which has long passed.

The market is neutral ground. Not his estate. Not my forest.

I make it a few meters before I stop again. I'm on the border of the abandoned marketplace. All the stalls have been pushed against the wide wall that surrounds it. No one has to worry about locking anything up; people don't steal here.

He is here somewhere. Waiting.

Grinding my back teeth out of habit, I keep my slow-crouch-walk going, hoping the street lamps' cones of light don't have the kind of range to reveal my position. The night that shrouds me is my only shield of protection against Alpha Rylan. If I had the resources, I would have an entire arsenal with me. Instead, I'm stuck with a thick sharpened piece of wood tucked into the back of my pants.

I don't know how this will go. Rylan surely will have brought his guards with him.

The marketplace shows itself as I walk only a few steps more. It is broad, having the ability to hold many people. I had expected to see Rylan right in the middle, waiting patiently for me. Instead, I see nothing. My eyebrows furrow.

The thing about Rylan is that I can't predict him. Not once have I understood his ability to do the unexpected so often. Usually, I have an uncanny knack at figuring people out, yet Rylan still remains under a haze of mystery. Sure, he sends his guards to find me pretty often, yet he somehow manages to *always* figure out where I am.

I hate being off guard. I should always have a plan ahead of time. Rylan offers me no space to create one.

I sit on top of the wall for at least five minutes.

The debate circling in my mind is a good one. My body tells me to turn and run, while my mind wants to lure me down there, to get a better look. For all I know, he could be around a dark corner I can't see from here. That, or his guards might be.

"I hate myself," I murmur, my whisper being caught by the soft breeze's clutches.

Turning my body around, I carefully maneuver myself until I am hanging with my stomach against the wall; my fingers clutching the edge are all that keep me from falling. Not that it would matter, since it's the only choice I have. When I let go, I land on my feet, but not without the jarring jolt of pain that spikes through my ankles and to my knees. Every day I do that.

The sound of my fall echoes, giving this place an even eerier feeling. I'm not scared of the darkness though. I'm scared of what might possibly be lurking in it.

I walk forward, the moonlight lighting everything in front of me. Rylan surely is the master of anticipation. I've set myself up on a platter for him. If he decides to swoop in and capture me, then so be it. If he thinks that will make me yield to him like a mate would, then he is utterly mistaken.

The cold crawls up my arms as I wait. I'm not going to announce anything. If he is here, then he knows.

He decides to show himself only seconds later.

I forgot how beautiful he is.

The moment he steps from the shadows, I have to exhale all the pent up anxiety in order to actually stay on my feet. I've decided it's his eyes that I can't ever get used to. A beautiful shade lighter than the average blue color. As he gets closer, I realize that it's a

3

silver ring on the outside that captures the shade of unimaginable blue within.

He's different from what I remember. He wasn't as... tall. Well built. Mouth water-

What am I thinking?

Instinctively, I straighten my shoulders and hold my ground. My confidence is all I have right now, however, this man is my mate. My knees weaken at the sight of him.

The last time I saw him, his hair was slicked back, he was slightly shorter and his muscles less defined. Now, he is a completely different person. He still dresses elegantly, with his dark trousers and pressed button down shirt. The rest of him is mussed and raw. His dark eyebrows disappear beneath a ruffled fringe of hair, framing his eyes.

I want to know what happened to the man I was running from. Who is this?

"Dawn," he whispers.

No matter how badly I want to look away, I keep my gaze sharp on him. His height is what has thrown me off-guard right away, along with his change in his appearance. He has to be able to look at me and see the same girl he saw years ago. Well, a forest-born version of me.

"Alpha Rylan," I say carefully, my quivering voice sounding strange as it dances along the concrete walls around us.

He shakes his head at me, looking at me from under his hairline. "I told you not to call me alpha."

I'm not like him or anyone in his pack. Born in the desirepack, I lived a life of freedom and excitement all through my teenage years, with the ability to make my own decisions, what with my parents working full time. Then we had to move to the purity pack, after my mother read an article about the moon goddess and decided she wanted to believe in her.

I tried to obey. But turns out I'm not very good at it.

4

They wanted me to go a boarding school which was targeted around religious studies for those who had just moved into this pack. It's not that I don't believe in the moon goddess, it's the fact that I cannot handle everything that comes with it. The rules. Rules don't sit well with me, I have learned. So, my sister and I ran away, narrowly missing being sent away for four years of our life.

That was when I met Rylan.

"That's all you are to me," I say softly, the bite in my words not there. Despite enjoying the distance from my mate, I found him passing through my mind every day. I never told my sister though. There was no point in worrying her.

In her wild little mind, she thinks I'm sick from having this space apart from him. I feel fine.

"I missed you," he whispers, the light from the streetlamps shimmering through his hair, giving it a lustrous golden tinge. I only really notice the little things about him.

Swallowing, I run my hands back across my thighs. "That's not what I am here to talk about."

Rylan looked sad for a moment, and my heart attacked itself.

It hasn't been my intention to purposefully hurt him. It isn't my fault he doesn't understand, no matter how many times I try to tell him. His life is made up of rules and religion, whereas mine is of freedom and choice. As much as he wants to make decisions for me, it's a deal breaker. My life isn't ready to be pinned down.

That is why I am here. To finally end this feud between us. He needs to let me go....

"Of course," he murmurs. "I suppose you're seriously considering leaving after this. I suppose you didn't need to think about it either."

My eyes automatically narrow on my mate in front of me. Perhaps he hasn't changed. He still looks at me in the same way; like some creature he doesn't understand. How could he? I'm a complete lunatic to someone as proper as him. His looks have changed, and so has his demeanor. Yet he still acts like I need a cage around me.

5

I hate that.

"Alpha, this is me you're talking to. You don't know much about me, but you do know I can't live your life. We are from separate worlds-"

"I'm willing to change," he says quickly, stepping farther forward into the light. I match his step backwards, nervous of his approach. "Will you please think about it? I can't be without you for another second."

His words are desperate, coming out rushed and forced. Another step forward. Another step back.

I begin to panic. What is his plan? Is he going to keep coming at me until I'm pressed against the wall back there? If so, I'm going to have to make a run for it, but first, I need to make sure he will stop sending men after me. The crazy male has an obsession for pursuit, and I don't think I could handle another year of enduring it.

"I have thought about it," I tell him warily.

"You're not well. I look at you, and I see how malnourished you are. Will you not let me take care of you?"

I shake my head. "No, Rylan... Alpha, I mean. I can't do it, I won't let you ship me off to one of your sick boarding schools. I'm done trying to be convinced."

Turning my back on him, I walk towards the massive wall I plan to scale over. Actually, I plan to have Rylan turn me around and agree to this deal. That's in a perfect world though. Unfortunately, I wasn't in one of them.

"Dawn!"

I pause.

Turning around, Rylan is staring at me. His eyes have darkened to a point where he looks like a member of the vengeance pack; cruel, merciless, and cold. The man of high morals is gone, and the same man who relentlessly sent those guards after me is there. I watch his jaw clench.

"I knew you would do this. I knew my stubborn girl wouldn't change," he murmurs, jarring my heart to a stop.

"Neither have you. That's why I'm leaving."

He shakes his head, and a flicker of guilt graces his eyes for a moment. That's how I knew things weren't going to end very well for me.

"It's dangerous out there, Dawn. No place for my mate," he says carefully.

I glance around, seeing guards emerge from the shadows. Each of them armed aptly, each wearing a set of armour that glints under the splinters of silver moonlight glaring down from the sky. All of their faces are hooded, as if they are in great danger of being seen by me. Am I really that terrifying in their eyes?

"I hate you," I growl, turning back to Rylan. He has blocked all my possible exits with his guards.

Guilt creeps into his expression now. "I had to, you're my mate."

"I hate you."

Two guards grab my arms, and I don't bother fighting back. What would be the point? I know for a fact that I don't have a possible escape in mind, so I am forced to be captured by him. But not without letting him know how I feel.

"I hate you," I repeat viciously.

I see the conflict there, but as the guard snaps the cuffs on my wrists, I cringe. The cool metal digs against my skin, but it's not that that hurts me. It's the feeling of finality that consumes me ... the feeling of being trapped.

"You have to understand. Baby, please," Rylan almost begs.

He stops talking as he sees the heat in my glare, the tears growing in my eyes. The betrayal.

"I *hate* you."

Chapter Two

It took me at least two minutes to figure out where I was when I next opened my eyes.

I haven't stared at a ceiling in a long time. There has also never been something so comfortable and soft underneath me, or warm wrapped around me, since I ran away. The feeling is awfully daunting, and for a good moment, I am paralysed. And not from the drugs Rylan's little team must have fed me last night.

I sit up slowly, rubbing a mildly aching head. This is the first time I have let Rylan get to me. I shouldn't have gone in for the meeting.... I know better than that.

Sliding my legs out of bed, I look down and cringe.

I've been put in a silky white nightgown made of pure satin. It reaches to my mid-thigh, the trim pasted with baby blue lace. It breathes the purity pack and all Rylan's wealth that he is willing to waste on a fugitive. What did he do with my other clothes? I only have two different pairs which I switch between every few days.

My wrists are slightly raw from the handcuffs, although, I'm glad they weren't silver.

As I stand, I look around the room. Honestly, I expected him to throw me into some dark prison out of fear or keep me handcuffed. Instead, I have been gifted a beautiful room. My feet, which haven't touched the soft strands of carpet in a year, are as grateful as my eyes as they register the comfort of the room. Four walls and the windows surrounding me are enough to remind me of what I left behind.

As much as I miss the comfort, I feel on edge. There is no way I'm staying here any longer than I have to. I'm getting out of here now.

Grabbing under the ridge of the window, I try to heave it up. Of course, it's locked. Glancing around, there are two doors in this small room, the only other items are a dresser and small desk. The color scheme is a white and a simple blue, like the lace on my gown. I wander to the first door and it opens easily.

It's a bathroom. Another common commodity I have lived without.

The tiles feel cool under my feet as I step into the lavish room. I try to imagine this building from the outside, after all the times I have observed it. His estate is almost as large as the forest that borders it, which leaves me little room to fully determine whereabouts I am within it. This also limits my ability to escape. If I am east of the building, I have no chance to get past his guards.

I allow myself a few seconds to admire the shower that looks a lot more inviting than the river I am used to before I check the second door. Convinced it isn't going to work, my heart falls, until it opens with the slightest touch.

Am I dreaming? Was it *really* Rylan who took me or a kinder soul?

Wandering out, I really have no idea of where I am going. I take a few doors here and there, but every time I am back in a hallway that looks exactly the same as every other one I have seen. Eventually I become so painfully lost that I begin hitting every wall I pass; I'm so close to banging my head on it instead.

Perhaps this is Rylan's sick version of torture. Have me wander around aimlessly until I go borderline insane. It's working.

Coming to a stop, I exhale and feel defeat, before sliding my back down the wall, my head falling into my hands.

"Giving up already?"

For whatever reason, Rylan's voice didn't startle me. He leaned against the wall in a casual manner, watching me curiously with those crystal eyes. How long has he been standing there for? How long has he been mocking my defeat as I press myself into the wall to avoid continuing down these infuriating hallways?

"Leave me alone," I growl irritably. "If you're not letting me out of this place, then I don't even want to see you."

Instead of dealing with him, I should be finding my way out. Now I'm lost and under his ridicule.

He sighs deeply, moving to walk in front of me. I can be very stubborn at times. I meet his gaze, making sure to hold it firmly. This man will not get the better of me here, even if it is his territory. He cheated in this sickening game of cat and mouse, and he's supposed to be the alpha of purity.

Purity my ass.

"I know this is hard-"

"Hard?" I spit in disbelief. "You tricked me and lied to me and dragged me here against my will to be your little pet. Fate did a terrible job pairing us together."

Rylan bit the edge of his lip as he thought. My breathing is rough around the edges as I try read his expression. All I can see is the impassive features that spell out nothing to me. He is too busy mulling over my words, watching me intently.

"You're not well, Dawn. I'm doing this to keep you safe, before you get even sicker from the life you're forcing onto yourself," Rylan says carefully.

I grit my teeth together.

"I look at you, and it pains me," he continues. "Seeing you deteriorate in front of me. You don't deserve that."

His words send heat through my veins. I'm not sure if I should be angry at him, or if I should just accept it, since I've been considering that for quite some time. Recently, I haven't been the same in my climbing, running and stealing. I've been getting sick. What if Rylan's words are true? Who knows what will happen to me?

"I'll feel better when I'm back home, with my sister," I tell him, knowing at least that much is true.

10

Lucy is only ten years old, and she's alone out there. If I hate myself for meeting Rylan, I hate myself for leaving her more. She's strong though; she will be fine on her own.

Rylan looks thoughtful. "You could always bring her here...."

"Not an option."

Rylan hasn't met Lucy yet. Lucky him. She's hates him more than she hates the idea of living in a forest, with fallen leaves for bedding and a stream for a bath. My poor sister is forced to retaliate against plenty of the guards he sends for me.

"Why not? Don't you want her to be safe?" Rylan questions, his eyebrows creasing. Him being this close to me makes me a little nervous.

Naturally, I'm attracted to Rylan. There is no denying that fact.

The mate bond - no matter how much I dislike it - is something undeniable. Fate chose Rylan to be the one who I crave and yearn for. I've been trying every day to prove that wrong.

"She doesn't want to be locked up, forced to pray to a goddess she doesn't believe in," I tell him forcefully.

"I've told you, I don't expect that from either of you," he tells me softly.

Lies.

"You have proven that you like me locked up, in an unfamiliar place, and all alone. You haven't given me a reason to trust you yet," I tell him honestly, raising an eyebrow.

He smoothly stands, before he holds his hand out to me. I stare at it.

"Come on, you must be hungry. When was the last time you ate something decent?" Rylan asks, his eyes filling with warmth; the first semblance of realism I have seen on him so far. Otherwise, he is a cold alpha who would rather see me locked up and kept pretty like a doll.

I'm not going to touch him. It might just ruin me.

So, I stand by myself, using the wall behind me as leverage. I feel a little nervous being dressed so inappropriately around Rylan,

11

however, I'm not completely uncomfortable. Still, I want my old clothes back.

"Fine, I'll eat, then I'm leaving," I tell him. I may as well get something from this, right? Maybe I can even steal something to bring back to Lucy.

Rylan smiles slightly. "We'll see about that."

The place seems completely abandoned as Rylan walks me through his house until we make it to an eating area. Does he live here alone? He allows me to sit at the head of the table, even pulling the oaken chair out for me. Manners don't exist where I've been.

"Feeling like anything in particular?" Rylan asks over his shoulder as he walks toward the kitchen.

With my hand folded over my lap, I quickly check the room for exits. None, unless I count the door we came from, but I saw nothing on our walk. Perhaps I could jump out the massive stained glass window with my shoulder as a shield against the glass. It would take less than a few seconds for him to find me again though …

"Food," I say and Rylan chuckles.

While he gets my food, I sit there like a proper lady would, taking myself by surprise. Anarchy would be simple to start right now, but I'm planning on gaining this alpha's trust.

Rylan walks back in, visibly surprised to see me still sitting here. He slides a plate of food in front of me.

"So, what happens now?" I question, after taking my first bite of the fresh fruit he has supplied. Being the first real food that isn't dried fruit and stale bread for quite some time, I relish in the delicious taste.

Rylan sighs. "We sort things out between each other. We find your sister. "

"What if I told her I didn't know where she is?" I say coyly, swallowing a spoonful of grapefruit flesh.

"I wouldn't believe you."

Rylan and I stare at each other for a moment, wordlessly. As much as his eyes are easy to get lost in, the anger within me keeps everything quelled.

"Listen, this isn't going to work. You can't keep me here as your mate, without me wanting to escape every moment of the day," I tell him firmly.

Rylan has a talent for switching moods in an instant. One minute he's calm, and soft and the next he is hard and cold. Right now he looks angry and with good reason. It's not the kind expression that angry normal people have though. This look is distant, and brooding. It suggests that he's thinking up some wicked things in his mind.

"I don't want to do this, however, I have little choice," Rylan says carefully. "I'm trying to help and protect you. I want you to have a good life, in safety and health."

"If you cared about me, you wouldn't hold me down," I tell him.

All of a sudden, Rylan reaches for me, but I flinch back. Respectfully, he retracts his hand.

"I do care, Dawn," he says smoothly. "Let me show you how much."

13

Chapter Three

Dawn

"As if."

"Come on...."

"No."

"Why not?"

I sigh. "I said no."

"That's not an answer."

A year was enough time for Rylan to become even more infuriating. Right now, he has decided he wants me to accompany him to dinner tonight, at some fancy restaurant he enjoys. Personally, sitting in an enclosed space with pompous people does not appeal to me.

I explain my thoughts to him, and he responds with a rather coy smirk. I knew he wouldn't understand. What I have gathered from him so far is that he enjoys watching me squirm with wariness about everything he puts in front of me. Honestly, I believe he has become too accustomed to having me in his possession.

However, I'm still thinking of a way to change that.

"Go on, Dawn," Rylan insists. "Someone has already drawn a bath for you."

A low growl rumbles in my throat. Being told what to do doesn't really sit well with me. Rylan is just a privileged alpha of purity, who fails to act like one. If anything, he should be sporting white all the time and have a few doves perched on his shoulder.

That was how I always imagined him anyway.

Not this tall, slender, yet rather defined male who enjoys wearing the sleekest black clothes that accentuate his waistline and broad shoulders.

"I'm doing this because I *want* a bath," I tell him, poking his chest threateningly, although he only smirks. "*Not* because you told me too."

I turn on my heels, glad to confirm with Rylan that I'm remaining stubborn.

He was right when he said someone had drawn a bath for me. Not only that, but the strange porcelain thing I haven't seen in a very long time has been dressed even better than me. Sweet little rose petals float like miniature sailboats across the expanse of the water. Even a subtle scent of roses and lavender wafts up.

I had to scour the ensuite to make sure whoever had created this small masterpiece wasn't hiding in my room somewhere before I could safely undress.

I did so slowly, letting the gentle satin kiss my limbs on its way off my body.

I should be grateful Rylan is giving me some space, at least. If he was demanding me to stay in his room with him, I think I may have committed to the consequences of first degree murder. As I dipped my foot into the bath water - the warmth sending a shiver up my leg, and to my spine - I mentally thank Rylan for his wealth and ability to pamper me, even if it does make me feel a little guilty. Poor Lucy.

Slowly, I let my bare body sink into the silky water; the scent wrapping around me like vines of utter pleasure, dragging me down, until my shoulders are completely submerged, and my neck rests on the edge of the bath.

Okay, this I can deal with.

The water doesn't feel brittle and icy like it did in all the streams I bathed in. Also, there's a lack of mud and slime underneath me, with an absence especially, of a stick in my back. And don't forget the roses and lavender. None of those exotic flowers grow in the forest.

"Oh Rylan." I breathe. "I'll never tell you this, but thank you."

Never would I give him the satisfaction of hearing those two words. *Ever.* As soon as I can, I'm going to get out of this place, but first ... I think I might just enjoy this bath.

My mind didn't register the fact that I had fallen asleep, until I woke.

The water around me had cooled, and my entire body had slipped down, until I was lying completely within the water, my ears submerged in the delicate water. Instantly, I started, sitting up, dragging my heavy, wet hair along with me. How long was I asleep? Long enough for the water to cool and my skin to wrinkle around my fingers.

A knock on the door startles me. "Hey ... you all right in there, Dawn?"

Rylan. Damn you, Goddess.

"Ah, yeah," I say breathlessly, standing in the bath. "Could you just give me a minute?"

Rylan may be surprised that I was using a kinder tone, and actually being a little more accommodating of his presence, but I'm blaming it on my very sudden awakening. I'm also stark naked, and not safely sure that I locked the door before I stripped.

There were no further words from Rylan, however, I hear his retreating footsteps.

Picking up a thick, soft towel, I step out of the bath to dry myself off thoroughly. How I wish I hadn't fallen asleep, because now my hair is soaking wet, and as much as I rub it furiously with the towel, I can't seem to get it close to dry.

When I wander out into the bedroom, towel wrapped around my body, I'm surprised to see Rylan sitting on the edge of the bed.

16

The window behind him lets in the gentle stream of subtle oranges and golds from the sunset. How long did I sleep for? Already, Lucy is going into her first night without me, and the guilt only seeps deeper into my every pore.

Rylan, however, doesn't seem fazed by that. The shadows from the window shape his jawline, making him look somehow sinister, even though he had shock written all over his face. And I know why... He stares at my hands that are pressing my towel to my chest, before they drift down to my bare legs, slightly dripping from the water I didn't get to.

"Dawn," he whispers, his voice a little hoarse.

I'm not necessarily the most confident girl with my body. So having another male stare so directly at me makes me wary. It seems Rylan feels the same way, as his gaze sweeps up to my raised eyebrow, he feels the need to answer to my qualms.

"I'm not supposed to think so wickedly about someone," he tells me, his eyes like a window open into his emotions. Internally, he is beating himself to the core, trying to teach his mind to be the perfect alpha of purity. My sudden ability to see this gives me a shock to my system as I think about what it really means.

There it is. His weakness.

He's my mate.... Of course I can see and feel these things, along with him.

"What are you thinking?" I can't help but ask in a soft whisper. In a single moment, I have been dragged down into his spell of enchantment.

He instantly shakes his head. "Nothing I am allowed to ... there has been a dress left for you. I hope you like it."

And just like that, he is out the door.

I'm left, in all my towel-like glory, to think over what in the world just happened. There was a part of Rylan that was being respectful to his religion, not wanting to have those thoughts that the goddess wouldn't like, until we were mated. There was another part of him struggling to control that, wanting to succumb to his natural advances.

Perhaps if I was interested at all in pursuing our relationship further, then maybe I would have had a bit of fun, trying to tear down that wall of self-control that he's built.

The dress that has been chosen for me to wear is mouth-watering. The fabric is a rich, royal blue color, with a bodice that perfectly sculpted in curves I didn't have; having lost them after a life in the forest. For a moment, as I slip the dress on, watching the gemstones glittering lustrously as they hit the light, I feel beautiful. I wasn't that sickly girl anymore.

In that moment, I am strong. And I can get through this.

Lucy played in my mind, as I parade back down the stairwell, my dress sashaying around my ankles almost dangerously. Like a proper gentleman, Rylan is waiting for me by the main door, and I almost had forgotten that I'm a kidnapping victim.

"Wow," Rylan says, a bewildered expression gracing his features. "You look stunning."

I've never been the kind of girl to try make herself look better than she actually does. If things look good on me, then that is a bonus, however, my wet hair suggests I don't really care. I can't let him see me break down any further into his spell of being his mate.

"You too," I say, my tone bland, yet I know I mean it. I can't help but admire how impressive he looks in a suit, and how he manages to make it look so casual, yet so proper at the same time.

He holds his hand out to me. He's wearing gloves.

It shouldn't have taken me by surprise. Gloves are a common fashion feature to every male's outfit. We haven't touched in over a year. No sparks for *that* long. He is protecting himself from what he felt earlier in the bedroom.

He loops his arm through mine, opening the door for me. The night air is like a cool slap in the face at first, as I imagine Lucy without my body heat.

As we step outside, I get a feel for where we are a little more. The courtyard that is well-lit has an elegant sports car parked there, with one door open to reveal a leather interior. It's a daunting sight, since my only mode of transport for this past year has been my two feet and no shoes.

Rylan leads me outside, seemingly calm. I could rip away from him right now and make a break for it. Is he not worried about me shifting and potentially escaping his grasp? Of course not, he would easily catch me.

"Careful," he murmurs, as I clamber uneasily into the car. Inside, it smells heavily of the leather that coats it, and for a moment, I feel a little light-headed. If possible, I would have done something to get away from this situation, to get back to my little sister.

"Where are we going?" I decide to ask, not wanting to be kept in the dark any longer.

Rylan smiles slightly, and the expression lights up his handsome features. "It's a small dining place. Maybe you will like it."

I didn't say anymore until we arrived. The place wasn't in the main central business district, or even close to the city. It was a modest little restaurant that was hardly populated by anyone tonight, and seeing it makes me a little excited, yet my stomach will most likely disagree. This kind of food may be too rich for me to handle.

Rylan helps me out of the car, making sure not to let go of me for a single second, so no opportunity can arise for me to make an escape. He shouldn't be worried about that in this dress…

When we make it to the door, Rylan pauses.

"Tonight, you're mine again," he whispers in my ear, before he swings the door open.

Chapter Four

Dawn

The restaurant is beautiful.

It has been too long since I have had a taste of what civilisation looks like, but wealth? This place may be simple and quaint, yet I still see the little things that make it worth more than I could ever fathom. From the richly colored table to the classic and opulent works of art strung on the wall, it made sense that this is one of Rylan's favorite places to go.

The warmth from the blazing, crackling fireplace to my left makes me aware of how warm it is in here. Shackles of heat wrap around my wrists, making me increasingly nervous.

I feel Rylan's hand on the small of my back. "Shall we sit?"

The queasy feeling building in my stomach wants to be expressed, however, I keep my mouth firmly shut. If I say something, I may anger Rylan, and that isn't going to get me any closer to Lucy. My poor little sister must be freezing outside, and hungry too. Guilt fills my gut.

"You look worried," Rylan notes, as he pulls a chair out for me to sit on. I do so quickly, making sure my outfit fits perfect under the table.

Rylan sits in front of me, gently pushing a vase of pretty purple flowers out of the way, so he can see me properly. Every time I look at him, I see an alpha who has never had to fight for what he wants. He has never been exposed to the horrors of life outside a pack, and how a lack of family can do so much to damage you.

I have to keep reminding myself that it is my fault. My decision to leave them.

"I wonder why," I mutter, looking down at my hands bunched in my skirt. Meeting Rylan's gaze may just tear a hole through the facade I have been wearing tightly around me.

He sighs. "I'm willing to compromise."

At his words, I decide to look up. His silvery blue eyes are like a veil, hiding something behind them that I wish to uncover. The steely expression on his face matches the color of his irises, yet he still manages to seem indifferent. What would he do if I slapped the impassiveness from his expression? Would he slap handcuffs on me again?

Is he afraid of me?

"I don't believe you," I say confidently, placing my hands on the table in front of me. "I don't believe you can change your ways."

Rylan seems to think carefully about my words. When I first met the alpha, he was strict in his ways of possession and protection. His belief in the moon goddess made him all the more hardened and forceful about his way, which made me especially uncomfortable. He's even shy about touching me, as if I might give him the worst form of sin like some disease.

"I'm trying," he says hoarsely. "I really am trying."

I don't believe him. "If you really wanted to change, you wouldn't have cornered me and kidnapped me. You would have accepted that I don't need you anymore. That I am better on my own."

Rylan sits forward on his seat, looking torn. Had I not seen it in his eyes, I would have been worried by the lack of expression on his face. He's good at wiping that away, like a whiteboard.

"I did it for your own good, don't you see that?" he says, almost desperately. "You are sick and getting worse. I can handle it, as an

21

alpha, but you on the other hand ... Do you really want your sister to have nobody when you eventually waste away? I would have been happy to bring her in, however, I would follow not long after you."

I shake my head at him. "I don't think you understand. I am not willing to be held captive here. I can't even begin to believe in your religion. If it means I get sick, then so be it."

My stubborn side has been released, and Rylan is left to try and simmer it down. My hands ball into fists on the table.

"At least tell me where your sister is," Rylan says softly, biting his lip distractedly. "So I can save her."

Fate pulls his strings at that exact moment.

A loud and almost deafening crash sounds from behind me. The sound of shattered glass skittering across the floor has me turning around in fear; the beautiful restaurant we saw originally has been destroyed and replaced by destruction. The sight of it all would have previously frightened me, but the shards of glass are like glittering stars of hope as I realize who has caused them.

Lucy. My precious sister

Standing on the other side of the broken window, in all her ten-year-old glory, is my sister clad in dark leather clothes, which I had never see her wear before. Her light blonde hair is slung up in a braid, her eyes glaring furiously over a black cloth that she has tied to cover half her face. She's used a brick to smash the window.

Neither me, nor Rylan has a chance to move, before Lucy comes behind me, the blade of a knife pressed threateningly close to my neck. I suck in the deepest breath, my gaze finding Rylan.

He looks indifferent at what he's witnessing, not saying a word.

"Put the knife down," he says calmly, looking as if he isn't fazed by this at all. I know that this is really his alpha-like experience coming out. He doesn't want Lucy to make a move to hurt me. He clearly has no idea that this strange, small girl is my sister. To him, she could just be someone out to hurt the alpha's mate.

22

Lucy has a short amount of time to get out of here before the staff who are tucked behind the tables call the police.

She doesn't say a word, not wanting to give Rylan any further hints of her age.

"This girl is innocent. I suggest you stop before you do something you might regret," Rylan continues, slowly standing, keeping his palms flat against the table. In any other situation, I would be glad for his negotiation skills, but now, I want to be far away from them.

Lucy's voice isn't her own, as she says, "Move another inch and she's dead."

The painted look of fear across my face is like an alert symbol for the alpha, which stops him from doing something he might regret. As I see the flash of fear in his eyes, of losing me, guilt sets heavy in the pit of my stomach. Lucy couldn't have known any other way to get me out of here, but it still makes me a little irritated that she had to threaten my life in front of him.

Slowly, with Lucy's body prompts, I am forced to my feet. Rylan only watches, eyebrows creased. He feels powerless, I can see. If he moves, he believes it may get me killed.

"I'm sorry," I choke out, unable to stop myself.

I feel the bond between us protest. When I felt it before it was a strange, painful feeling in my stomach that I dealt with for an entire week before I could feel better again. Now, the disgusting, incriminating feeling creeps back with every step I take backward. I try to suppress it.

Lucy may have been shorter than me, but the boots she was wearing gave her enough height to match mine, which was enough to lead me over the glass window. My foot almost catches on the sharp shards that stick out dangerously, but I didn't look down.

There was no way I could have been able to take my eyes off Rylan. Especially his darkening eyes, as he remained sitting at the table in the middle of the room.

"I'll get you back," he says softly, knowing there was no way to get out of this. "I'll tear the world apart."

And that was the last sentence I heard from my mate, before Lucy and I escaped into the darkness of the streets.

***

"What was it like inside?" Lucy asks, her inquisitive smile wide.

We didn't say a single word to each other, until we had made it back to our original camp. It was too dangerous, as we kept close to the walls, until we made it out over two hours later. Unfortunately for my weakened legs and awkward dress, the walk was painful, but Rylan's house was on the other side of the pack, and we couldn't change that.

"No," I dismiss carefully, stoking the fire with the edge of a blunt stick. "You have to tell me how you found me."

Lucy is strong; I've always known that. Yet, I had no idea she was capable of organising such a successful rescue mission from an alpha. The poor girl should be in school right now, brushing other girls' hair and doing their makeup. Not living in a forest with her messed up sister every night.

She sits in front of me in the dirt, her legs stretched in front of her and covered by a tattered blanket we have had since we first ran away. The firelight licks up her pretty features, darkening her already almost black eyes. Her hair has darkened since we have been out here, but it has always been so golden and beautiful.

"I followed you," she tells me smoothly. "I knew you were going to meet with him. You couldn't help yourself."

Sometimes Lucy makes me feel inferior to her. She slowly chews on the edge of a loaf of bread we stole from a closed market stall on our way back, staring at the dress I wore.

"You know me too well."

"Yes, well ... now you can tell me what it's like-"

"Hold on," I say, holding my hand up to stop her. "You followed me to Rylan's estate? Where did you sleep that night?"

Lucy seems irritated at my lack of answers for her question. "Slept in his wine cellar."

24

"All right, well, inside his home is amazing. He is very wealthy, and owns some amazing things. You would have loved it, had it not been the most oppressive and monitored place in this entire world. You would have dug a hole through the wall soon enough," I tell her.

She seemed crushed at my words, but she expected it. I know for a fact that she doesn't want to live Rylan's life as much as I don't. It's the biggest reason why I haven't handed myself to him.

I stand while Lucy watches me. Slowly, I unzip my dress from the back and shrug it off.

During these cold nights, I could do with the extra fabric. Right now though, I want a symbol to thank Lucy with, so I stand, taking the dress I took off, to throw into the fire.

The flames swallow it in a second, sparks flying up, as the fire hungrily engulfs every inch of the expensive fabric. Lucy watches it silently, a content smile on her face, as what was once beautiful slowly turns into nothing but ashes.

"He won't ever find us. It's over now," Lucy murmurs.

For some reason, I don't believe her. She mustn't have seen the look in his eyes in those last moments.

And at that moment, I couldn't be so sure.

Chapter Five

Dawn

He leans against the thick base of the tree like prey.

My mind plays with ideas, as my eyes follow the line of the slightly quivering bow in my hands. It's handmade and not all that reliable. It will do the job though, if I decide to completely blow my cover. It might be worth it though, to see him in pain, even if it's for a flicker of a second.

He was wearing his dark leather outfit, created especially for Rylan's guards. They never used to wear the bulletproof clothing, or wear hoods over their faces. They never were from the power pack either, where some of the most elite soldiers were trained. I remember when they were incompetent purity pack members who were too scared to hurt anyone.

It has all changed since I escaped Rylan for the second time, three months ago.

I pull the string of the bow back and hear it groan very slightly by my ear. It's not often that I use the bow and arrow, which I made messily, but today, I need to put a little unease into these highly trained law enforcers. They have been hanging around in the wrong part of the forest, not near Lucy and me, so I have decided to send this arrow at them to make them think they are on the right track.

That's my theory anyway. I'm not sure if they will actually catch on, since they are all brawn over brains.

The arrow hits him exactly where I had anticipated. Right in the foot.

I only give myself a single moment to rejoice in my perfect hit before I pull my mask of leaves across my body. Being in a tree is a more dangerous way to stalk the guards, but it gives me a good vantage point at least. I can see perfectly, as the Elite doesn't move a single inch. His eyes fell down to the arrow in his foot, not making a single sound, like I had expected him to.

His lack of reaction makes me nervous, as he pulls the arrow from his foot without a moment's hesitation. A sheen of blood glints off of it, confirming that it had gone in, yet he acted as if it hadn't, letting his shoe keep the wound in.

Then he casts a dark gaze up to where I am in the tree.

I don't move an inch.

He can't possibly see behind these leaves, so he shouldn't know I am hiding behind here. I even hold my breath, seeing those cruel, shallow eyes look between the leaves. Then, he snaps the arrow in half, and turns to his small group who had been silently watching him. They knew not to speak until commanded to.

"She's here," the elite muttered, his voice low, as if to conceal it from me. I did though, and I was quick to turn to the trunk and scale down the tree so quickly that my arms scraped against the bark viciously until blood was drawn.

As my feet touched the ground, I turned to see myself surrounded by the elite guards.

They are a lot more intimidating than they once were three months ago. I've managed to avoid them at all costs, but now, as they stand in front of me, I have no other choice but to accept their presence.

Leather clad weapons are strapped to their sides and masks cover half their faces. They are terrifying. An unfamiliar shiver of fear stalks up my spine, making me swallow dryly. This time, it's serious. The only common sense here is the fact that the leading Commander Burke still runs the show.

He stares at me with those brutish eyes.

"It looks like the tables have turned," Burke says, in the bloodthirsty tone I found painfully familiar. You wouldn't tell he prays on his knees to the goddess morning and night just by looking at him.

I keep my eyes on him, instead of his guards. Six of them this time.

"I found you this time," I say, knowing what he meant, just not wanting to admit it. It had been my idea to seek him out. I had no idea that he had brought such experienced reinforcement.

"You're not getting away," he tells me securely, his thin, dry lips curving into a malicious smile. "Unless you want every one of these men killed."

I force a shrug into my shoulders. "I wouldn't mind."

The impassive look on their faces remain, as they seem unbothered by my claim. They don't know me. They would usually be working in a difficult environment for the alpha of power, risking their lives to defend their pack's. Now, they work for the alpha of purity, risking their lives in another way. Now, they must be thought of as a joke, being hired to chase after an alpha's mate.

"These males have families. They have lives. You don't care that your mate will destroy them, before replacing them without a single thought?"

Is this his idea? Blackmailing me? He should have taken a different route if he wanted to sway me.

"I'm going to leave now," I say casually, taking a step backward.

The sweet song of native birds in the trees ceases, followed by gentle breeze that ruffles the leaves in the trees. Everything stops; even the clouds in the sky, as if they are watching, not believing the audacity of my statement. My sister would reply the same in this situation, so why can't I be brave?

Normal people would be on their knees in front of these elites by this point, but Commander Burke shakes his head at the males who step forward, gloved hands on their weapons.

28

"Don't. She's not going anywhere," he tells them, an air of confidence and spite around him that makes me nervous. "Not if she wants to know about her family."

I stop moving.

I left my family behind over a year ago. They haven't put nearly as much effort into trying to find me as Rylan has, which should have pained me, but it made me grateful. Their belief in the goddess is extreme, so them complying with whatever their puritan alpha has to say doesn't surprise me at all.

I'm still shocked into a pause.

"You changed him, you know. You two are perfect for each other," Burke says.

"We are opposites."

"Tell that to all the people he has killed over the past few months in cold blood. He's not pure anymore, girly. You've sickened him in the head."

I swallow, watching the tense muscles of the Elites, all of whom want to make a move. They haven't spent this many months in a forest looking for me, to just stand there and watch. Striking appeals to all of them, but they know not to step out of line of their commands.

"That's not my problem," I tell him, yet my tone quivers.

"You can take responsibility for the search going on for you. The time off work people have had to have. You can even be held accountable for all the innocent souls Rylan has tortured for information." Burke is enjoying telling me this.

There is little I believe about that. This isn't the weak alpha who only sent out the most pitiful guards for me. He *can't* have changed *that* much.

"He wouldn't," I say carefully.

"You doubt it, do you? Have you not seen the pack of peace turn into a frantic search for their luna? Be lucky they aren't brave enough to venture this far into the forest," he taunts. "They would drag you back to Rylan without a second thought."

29

Lucy and I have been living off the land, refusing to shift into our Wolves so Rylan wouldn't be able to sniff us out. It's been difficult, not visiting the pack for decent food at all, but we haven't had a choice.

It hasn't helped my sickness. I'm getting weaker by the day.

Slowly though, slowly Lucy and I have been stalking deeper into the forest. Our plan is to conceal ourselves to a point where no-one will even get close to us. We can live out our precious life of freedom away from all of them.

"Does this make you think I am going to just walk into his arms because of it?" I question, mildly disgusted by that notion.

If anything, it makes me frightened of him.

"He won't stop until he has found you. You're his mate, and an alpha's one too-"

"I didn't ask for it," I snap, unable to hold back my emotion.

They didn't seem to notice the step I had taken backwards, giving myself enough of a gap, that when I decided turn to run, they would have less of a chance to grab at me initially. If there is one thing I have on my side, it is my ability to run. I've always been quick on my feet, and I'm about to let that work to my advantage.

I can't stay here another second. Not with Rylan's words mulling in my mind.

I would tear the world apart to find you.

So I turned and I ran. Instantly, the elites were in pursuit, but they don't know the forest like I do. It takes me a few minutes of quick stepping and dodging around trees for me to lose them. When I do, I take a break, not knowing exactly where I am, but I know I'm close to our camp.

My heart pounds in my chest from my narrow escape, and my harsh breathing has my head spinning slightly. Resting my back against the bark, I wait for the mind whirling to stop.

But it doesn't…

I don't know how long I was passed out, but when I woke, the sun was setting and my face was buried in the dirt. Someone was at my shoulder, trying to push me onto my back. Blearily, I look through the slits in my eyes, seeing my concerned sister above me.

She is talking. "Something is seriously wrong with you. You need medicine, or at least good food."

My mouth is too dry to formulate any reasonable words as Lucy helps me to sit up against a tree. Still, despite my aching neck, I shake my head in protest.

But there is no doubting what is going to happen.

We are going back to the purity pack.

Chapter Six

Dawn

"This is a stupid idea," I grumble, flinching away from Lucy's touch. "I can hold up on my own for a while yet. Let's just get away from the purity pack-"

Lucy slapped me.

The sound echoes around the trees; the jarring feeling shocking some sense into me. She had given me three hours to recover after my near collapse in the forest. I had been lucky to get away from the elites in time, otherwise, I would have been locked up in Rylan's home with him, or maybe in a prison somewhere.

"You'll be dead in another few days," she growls as I rub my searing cheek.

A part of me knows she is right. My legs feel heavy and sluggish, and I know that if I had to make a run from another guard, I wouldn't make it. I don't know when the last time was that I ate a full, proper meal. Probably with Rylan ... Since then, it's been small morsels.

Lucy doesn't know I give her most of the food; she thinks it is evenly distributed. She matters most to me. If I hadn't dragged her away from freedom, she wouldn't be starving at most times of the day.

Now, we balance atop the massive wall that I'm used to climbing. Today though, it hurts having to pull myself up here with the little strength I have.

"We go in then straight out again," I mutter, casting a glance across the pack.

Admittedly, it looks beautiful tonight. The sky is free of all clouds, so the lights visibly sparkle under the glittering stars above. This is what I love about the outside. If I was deep within the center of the pack, I wouldn't be able to see a single thing up in the sky, with all the light pouring from it. I would rather sit up on this ledge and breathe in the sweet air.

Lucy hops down first, her feet making little noise compared to mine as she lands on the cobblestones of the market I'm very familiar with.

Both of us are dressed inconspicuously, so that we could keep to the shadows. I'd stolen these leathers off a guard I had managed to knock unconscious, making them loose around our limbs. They were enough to keep our skin hidden, especially with the addition of Lucy's cloth around our mouths.

The stalls are covered with beautiful striped cloth, keeping the food left over fresh for tomorrow. It's perfect for us.

However, when I lift up the first cloth I come up to, I'm surprised to see nothing but bare counter underneath. With a furrowed brow, I raise my head for Lucy to see. She is checking another stall, and she comes up with the same result.

Nothing.

Lifting every cloth to find no food was painful. My stomach ached at the sight, and my heart fell as desperation hit. This is Rylan's fault. His manhunt for me has made people nervous, and with all the rules he has enforced - from what I have heard - has caused wariness.

That and no food for us.

"We are going to have to delve deeper," Lucy murmurs, meeting me in the corner of the small marketplace.

It would be smart to grab her arm and leave here before one of Rylan's guards show up, but my protesting stomach demands that I find food elsewhere. Lucy seems content with the lack of my usual indignant attitude.

33

"We should split up and go to the two places we know where there *may* be food," Lucy says, glancing over her shoulder as if someone was coming up behind her. "Meet here in half an hour."

I learned how to gauge time pretty well in the forest, so this is not a difficult task. Still, I'm wary of leaving Lucy alone in a place probably swarming with guards, but she is street smart, and can look after herself. In my weakened state, she might just be better than me. I sometimes forget she is only ten years old.

We split, my sister slinking into the shadows of a nearby alleyway, while I keep to the walls, moving until I find a familiar opening in the wall, which I slip through.

It leads straight into a small street. I check that the coast is clear before walking out on to it.

The moon glints across the cobblestones, illuminating the sides of people's homes, with their doors locked and their curtains drawn. purity pack members are always afraid, which makes my job easier, since they should all be hiding away until dawn. The guards, on the other hand, are an issue.

I see three at the end of the street. Elites. They seem to have met up for a brief meeting before dispersing for another round.

I keep my back against the wall whilst I wait for an idea to come to mind.

I can't possibly go left, obviously, otherwise I'll be face to face with the Elites. But if I go to the right, there aren't any shadows for me to hide in, what with the streetlights tossing light everywhere the moon isn't. I have absolutely nowhere to go but back-

My thoughts were cut off, as a gloved hand suddenly covered my mouth.

I didn't scream, as they pulled me back, afraid the Elites might hear me. I can escape a predator in the night, but I know that there's no way I can fight my way out of this situation. So, giving the person behind me their victory, I let them drag me back through the wall I had just come through, and into the marketplace.

That's when I decided to strike.

34

The heel of my foot found their shin, while my elbow came back against their stomach. Usually, I would have stunned them enough to turn around to properly do some damage, but my captor didn't even flinch, nor make a sound. Instead, their grip remained tight on me.

They let me go, though, so I stumble backwards until I hit the wall. My captor is a man; his light hair sticking out from under his hood. He has a sickening smile spread across his pasty features, which had my stomach turning uneasily.

"Alpha's mate." He breathes darkly. He knows....

I shake my head. "Let me go."

It feels stupid to beg like that, but there is no way I can fight him. Usually, someone of his height and weight wouldn't be a problem, even if he is larger. In my state, however, being weaker than I ever have been, I don't think I would stand a chance. I have to talk my way out of this.

There are few purity pack members that break the rules, but every now and again, there are the few who want to break free of *all* the rules. This man is one of them; I can tell. He wants a little fun before he has to conform to his pack's society.

I just wish I could see what's running through his mind.

"You know what kind of reward I'm going to get for you?"

I'm not sure why he doesn't expect me to run from him, with the gap between us. He looks anxious, his hands trembling by his side. He regrets this. I could do him a favor and run, but I may just collapse again if I try.

"You don't want to do that," I say carefully, feeling as though I'm walking along a tightrope. "Seriously."

A flicker of anger streaks over his features. "You're the reason my alpha has gone crazy. You know he killed over you? I'm doing this pack a favor in this."

My heart sinks. It's hard to believe Rylan would ever kill. Can I even believe these rumors, or am I being manipulated without knowing it?

"My and the alpha's relationship is not something for you to worry about. Please let me go," I say, my quivering voice distracting enough for him not to notice the way I was slowly sidling across the wall. I knew that if I got close enough to the next exit, that Lucy had previously taken, I might be able to slip away undetected, and get him caught by a patrolling elite.

The man, who is starting to look more and more like a boy as time passes, runs his hands through the shocking mop of bright blonde hair on his head, until his hood falls back.

He's younger than me. Yet not by much.

"He's offering so much money for you, though." He breathes, looking conflicted. I want to say he has serious problems, but I keep my opinion to myself.

"Trust me, it's not worth it. Please. He wants to lock me up and force me into being a perfect luna. I think we have a lot in common in that regard. He may be all the way across the pack, but that male has eyes everywhere, which means I'm seconds from being captured by an elite. I beg for mercy."

My words seem fair, but the moment I finish my sentence, I regret it. I see the anger flame in his eyes.

He strides forward, and as his hand finds my neck, I begin pleading in my head to be found by an Elite. At least they wouldn't hurt me, knowing Rylan would have their head for it. This unruly man doesn't care. And he might just have intended to kill me, except the pressure on my neck isn't life-threatening.

"You know what my friends are going to say when I tell them I got a taste of my luna?"

My heart stops, and I swear I am on the brink of death from that alone. He plans to rape me? Here? With guards walking around who would have him slaughtered because of it?

Logic and reason spews out of my mouth in protest, as he pins me against the wall. He doesn't listen to a word of it.

If my mind hadn't been swimming, and my eyes were not blurred from hunger and sickness, I would have killed him myself. The knife tucked in the back of my pants is now unreachable. I didn't want to bring it out earlier, hoping I could convince him to do the right thing. Now, I'm regretting it.

"You don't want to do this," I say, as he grabs the front of my shirt with his free hand, ripping it straight down the middle.

My nakedness doesn't bother me. It's my impending fate that does. Speaking of fate, why does he have to be so cruel? This young male is going to rape me, and the moment Rylan finds out, he will be dead. You don't touch a male's mate, especially not an alpha's.

"I want you," he growls in my ear. He knows I'm not about to scream, but just in case, he slaps his hand over my mouth.

I'm alone and I'm about to get raped in an abandoned marketplace.

And there's nothing I can do about it.

Chapter Seven

Dawn

"You don't have to do this," I reason through his fingertips, my stomach turning at the feeling of the young male's lips against my neck.

He ignores me, his free hand roaming wildly across my body as he pins me against the wall. I'm done for. As he tightens the grip of his hand around my mouth, it dawns on me that there is no escape out of this. I am at his mercy, and that feeling may possibly be the worst I have ever felt.

That was until a hand came from the darkness behind him, and tapped his shoulder.

Already being on edge from what he was doing, the boy jumped away from me. I remained against the wall, wondering what was happening. Someone has saved me. Someone is wrestling him to the ground.

There was a single punch and it was over.

Looking to my left, I contemplate slipping away, undetected, before my savior can be another witness so Rylan's mate. However, I only take a single step before the mysterious figure stands, wiping his fist along his clothes. I can tell it is a male, with his broad shoulders and muscular arms. He covers himself in a dark trench coat, which is perfect for patrolling the night without being seen.

As he turns around, I realize instantly that he isn't from this pack, which is a relief.

His features are dark, with ebony eyes and obsidian black hair. His facial features are sharp and refined, and I recognise him as someone from the vengeance pack.

The purity pack's worst nightmare.

The two packs have been at war for a long time, and it was only recently that everything between them mellowed out. Still, it is very rare to see a vengeance pack member in the midst of the purity pack, since they don't follow their religion. In fact, they ridicule it for the most part. We have that in common.

He grinned slightly, noticing the way I was inspecting his gloves. They are leather and are gleaming with a sheen of blood from where they struck the boy's nose.

"You're welcome."

For whatever reason, it made me a little mad that he had done it. As grateful as I am, he's staring directly at my bare chest that I'm covering with my arms. I came from the desire pack, so I know a douchebag when I see one.

"I'm Kace, by the way," he tells me, holding his hand out. Noticing the blood, he quickly retracts it.

Maybe I should make a run for it. He may have saved my life, but who knows what he is going to do next. Being from a pack almost everyone despises, I'm apprehensive to be around him for another second. By the looks of him though, he's probably fit. In my state, I would make it a few meters, and he would catch me again. It's best to figure out what he wants.

"Thanks," I say softly. "I think I'm going to go."

Clenching my teeth, I begin a slow walk toward the escape, trying to make it look as if I'm not running from him. He follows me briskly, and I fight the urge to cringe.

"Let me escort you back to your home," he offers delicately. This time, I do cringe.

"We would be caught by an Elite in a few moments," I remind him, thinking of the swarm of them that would be out there.

Kace grabs my arm and I flinch. "Running from something?"

When I looked into his eyes, I had a feeling he knew *exactly* who I was. How could he not? Rylan has been parading pictures around of me to help people identify me, which suggests there isn't a person in this pack who doesn't know what I look like at this point. So, with Kace's coy comment, I have a feeling he is about to drag me over to an Elite for a reward.

"Only males who think it's okay to take advantage of innocent females," I mutter, resuming my walking. I'm hoping Lucy doesn't come back soon, otherwise she's going to be caught up in this.

"Lucky I'm not like that then," Kace comments.

I roll my eyes. "You were trying to look at my chest a few seconds ago."

"Only admiring ... Come on, it's cold out, and you need to get home. The elites and I ... well, we are okay with each other," he tells me, which makes me stop. At this point, I don't care about a ripped shirt, even though I still am covering my chest with my arms. I'm curious about this Kace guy and how he could possibly be 'okay' with the elites.

Or even how I could use that to my advantage.

"Okay fine, I'll let you take me home," I say carefully. In actual fact, I'm letting him help me pass the elites to go somewhere I can find food.

He offers his trench coat and I gratefully take it, wrapping its warmth around my body. He wore a dark shirt underneath, which clung to his chest, I noticed, but refused to look at it for more than a few seconds. I have no intentions of giving the coat back either, if I am perfectly honest. He looks wealthy anyway, so I don't see his need for it.

Turns out, the elites don't even look twice at us when I'm beside Kace. I keep my hair under the collar, my head down so they wouldn't recognize me. When we first glided past, I thought Kace would thrust me at them to claim the reward, however, he surprised me by making no move to do so.

"So, where do you live exactly?"

"This way," I murmur, pulling him down a small side road emanating the delicious scent of food. Right now I can't concentrate on anything else. If I don't eat something in the next hour then I'm sure I will collapse, and who knows what Kace will do then.

We pause outside a quaint little restaurant, having come around the back of it so as not to be seen. Kace seems confused, watching me while I begin to pick the lock of a door that I knew must lead to a storeroom. I work the lock with a piece of metal wire I found on the ground of the alleyway. I wish I could have shaken Kace a while ago, but he was keen to keep walking beside me, as if he were my pet.

"Wow, I'm witnessing a crime," he mutters, yet makes no move to stop me.

I hear the satisfying click of the lock. "You can go if you like."

He remains in his spot, much to my dismay. I'm risking being caught, but my want to find food for both me and Lucy is too high. Kace doesn't bother to say another word as I slowly open the storeroom door, hoping no one is inside. When I see my silent wishes have been answered, I exhale in relief.

Even a strange man from the vengeance pack can't ruin this.

Inside, I realize it's primarily a cool room for bread and cheese. I stuff some under the coat and wander back outside. Kace still stands there, watching me carefully with his hands shoved in his trouser pockets.

Either he has a lot of patience, or he is here for another reason.

"You don't have a home, do you?" he asks pointedly, and I shrug. The feeling is weird, with my pockets stuffed full of food. I just want to reach in and eat it now, but I refrain in front of Kace. He thinks I'm strange enough as it is.

I shake my head. "Look, you should probably go."

41

Kace watches me silently for a moment, as if he's about to say something, but he changes his mind. Something about him just seems too ... deliberate. I keep my mouth shut though. It's easier to shake him off before he finds out I'm Rylan's mate, if he doesn't already know.

He takes a few steps backward, the shadows of the alleyway almost eating away at him. "Keep the coat."

And then he was gone.

Shaking my head in disbelief, I take my time heading back to the marketplace where I knew Lucy should probably be waiting. It was much harder to evade the Elites but keeping to the shadows is something I know, and with a little luck, I manage to make it past the majority of the guards.

Slipping through the part of the wall that leads back, I pause. A loud, horrified shriek catches my attention.

Peeking my head around the corner, my heart skips at the sight.

"Tell me where Dawn is."

An elite has a girl by the collar of her shirt, having lifted her feet off the ground completely. I couldn't see much of her, apart from her brilliant shock of blonde hair. A typical purity pack feature. I have never seen her in my life, so why is the Elite threatening her? She won't know me at all.

"I-I have no idea... I swear," she begs, her voice laced with fear. I could imagine her crying, her fingers clawing at the hand he held her by.

"Don't lie," the elite growls, pushing her back so she stumbles back against the wall. "Tell me where she is, or you can deal with Rylan yourself."

There was a whimper. Rylan has to be doing something to these poor people to freak them out. If he dislikes Alpha Kaden of the vengeance pack so much for the terror he causes, he should probably look in the mirror. Right now, I'm fighting with an alpha, and with his attitude this awful, it means that I'm best hiding.

"I promise I haven't seen her. Someone is trying to get me in trouble!"

"Then why are you out here at night?"

A pause.

"I was going to visit my boyfriend. That has nothing to do with Dawn! I would give her in the second I saw her, I swear. I respect Rylan-"

The sound of her being slapped fills the alleyway, and I duck back into the wall. I need to go there and stop it. She doesn't know who I am, which means she doesn't deserve to be beaten by an Elite. They are such powerful and awful people...

"Dawn," I hear from behind me. "We need to go."

Lucy held my arm, gently pulling me away. Hot tears stung my eyes, as guilt consumed me. This is my fault. If I handed myself into him, then everything would be fine.

And for the first time in over a year, I'm seriously considering it.

Chapter Eight

Dawn

A few more weeks pass.

It got to the point where Lucy was going into the pack because it was too dangerous for me. Rylan has guards posted where we usually go in, and the amount of elites scouring the forest has almost tripled.

I hate him for it. He knows it too, since I told him.

"You're getting paler by the day," Lucy tells me one afternoon. She stands over me, the golden sun glistening in her dark hair.

I'm aware of how hopeless I look and how sickly and disgusting I am. Lucy looks tired, but other than that she is still my stunningly beautiful sister. Even if she looks a little ruffled, she's pink-cheeked, as if she's been running. She has been pursued numerous times, especially lately, however, she is too quick for them. Perks of being a ten year old, I suppose.

"Thanks," I mutter sardonically, grabbing the bread she holds out to me. "I can't help it, you know?"

Lucy sighs deeply, sitting on the log we've positioned by the fire.

"Sometimes I think you would be better off with Rylan," she tells me suddenly. I frown, not expecting her, of all people, to say that. She is the one who has kept me away from Rylan, thinking he isn't the best influence on either of us.

My teeth clench as I shake my head at my sister. "We are better out here. I'll be fine in a few days, and then we can begin our trek toward the freedom pack."

Collectively, we have decided to migrate to the freedom pack, where anyone can live without the alpha and luna finding out. It seems like a perfect idea, but the walk there will take us weeks, and I'm not sure how much strength I can muster to make it.

I won't tell Lucy that though.

"I'm excited about that, you know?" Lucy comments, realizing it's foolish to argue with me about this. "I think it's going to be fun."

She's right.... It will be nice not having to worry about being caught when finding food. I may even be able to get a job so we can have an actual house to live in, and she can go to school. Lucy is intelligent, but that wouldn't stop her from punching a kid in the face if they said something smart to her.

The thought of it makes me smile. She would be expelled on the first day.

"I'm going to make life good for you, I promise," I vow softly, and Lucy smiles, moving to sit beside me. Wrapping my arms around her, I bask in the feeling of the only one left in my life. One day, she will find a pleasant mate, because Fate cannot be so cruel, and she will leave me.

And I won't mind.

"I love you," she whispers against my shirt.

"I love you more," I murmur, and that was when he appeared.

First, I was shocked that I hadn't heard him coming. From my time in this forest, I have developed quite a keen sense when it comes to my hearing. Even Lucy, who is more talented than anyone I know, can't hear an animal's footsteps until it is right outside our camp.

The dark figure, who had previously watched from the trees, emerges so we can see his face.

45

Back in school, I didn't care less about learning the alphas' names, or even anything about them. I know about the alpha of vengeance, though. *Everyone* knows about Kaden.

Textbooks don't do mercy to the soulless shallows of his eyes; the ebony black swirling within in them seems to be made up of dark cruel memories ... and maybe even the souls of all his victims, however, that is just a part of the myths we told as bedtime stories. Something about them had shivers dancing down my spine.

They say when you see him, you're dead. He doesn't visit commoners for no reason.

He had this kind of casual smile on his face that I couldn't explain. He knows he has found who he is looking for; it's obvious from the look in his eyes. Honestly, I'm terrified, as I can think of nothing I have done that would cause Alpha Kaden to show up at our camp.

Unless ...

"Good evening, Dawn," he says carefully, in that melodic tone only vengeance pack members can master. It reminded of my savior from last night. Kace. I wonder what he is doing now.

I take a wary step backward, my heels hitting the edge of the log I had been sitting on. "How did you find me?"

There is a sinking feeling in my stomach, as my mind comes up with reasons why he may be visiting. He is almost like the symbol of death, ready to steal my life away for all the murderous sins I have committed.

There is only one death I've caused. The guard came at me with a Taser, and I was defending myself. I had no idea I would hit him the exact right spot to cause immediate death. I've hated myself ever since, but I don't talk about it. Only perhaps to Lucy, but she doesn't deserve to listen to her murderous sister.

"My brother, Kace. He helped me track you back here," Kaden comments.

Out of the corner of my eyes, I watch Lucy slip away, her body curving around the tree. Hopefully Kaden doesn't notice her sudden disappearance.

46

"You're wasting your time," I tell him, carefully watching my words so he can't twist them in a way that suits him. I know for a fact that he dabbles in riddles, which means I'm not about to make myself a player in his game.

He tilts his head. "How so?"

I wanted to bring up his mate. It was Lucy who found out that they had been in a relationship for nearly three years. She's a purity pack member, which makes it all the more scandalous in many people's eyes. I couldn't care less, but in this situation, I can use it as a bargaining chip. It's the only thing going for me against an alpha.

"Shouldn't you be home with your mate?" I say nonchalantly. "And your child?

His jaw clenches, his eyes darkening. Got him.

"That is none of your business," he seethes, however, his irritated expression morphs into an indifferent one, as if nothing I could say would affect him. His well-armored demeanor isn't something I can fight against.

He takes a small step forward, and I stumble back behind the log. "Please leave me alone. It was an accident."

"So, you admit it?" he says, his method of winding me up unfortunately working to his advantage. He has a delighted expression on his face that anyone would naturally want to slap off, however, there is no point. He would kill me on the spot, and I'm walking on eggshells as it is. "You admit that you murdered that innocent man?"

This time, I don't say a word.

"You know what I do to murderers?" he questions. He's like an animal playing with its food.

My stomach sinks once again, fear attacking my heart as it beats frantically. I want to turn and run, but something tells me I won't be able to escape someone like Kaden. The way he looks at me suggests he's reading every kind of idea I'm conjuring up.

I feel utterly hopeless. Just him looking at me strips me bare.

47

"I first have a few people decide whether or not you deserve to die," he tells me slowly, his lips tilting up at his own words. "If not, you will serve the rest of your life as a slave within my pack. Sometimes that's a death sentence ... or worse."

Again, I shiver, and not from the setting sun. The idea of being a slave is worse than any pain I would have to go through by being Rylan's mate.

I decide to take a different route. "It's been over six months. A little late on the game there, Alpha?"

He tilts his eyebrow up, not expecting retaliation.

"I was spending time with my mate. I suppose you can't say the same thing," he comments. It frightens me that he knows so much about my life already. "What are you so scared of? You could have some fun with him to... turn that pure mind into something as dark and disturbing as you."

That hurt a little, but I don't let it show. Rylan is too perfect for me. He deserves a submissive mate who will conform to his rules with no questions asked. He can't find that with me, and I have a feeling Kaden knows that.

"Rylan and I are not mates," I tell him confidently. "I think Fate made a mistake."

Kaden chuckles. "Fate, huh? That man does not make mistakes. Perhaps it was a practical joke on his part, but you will not find a trace of a mistake on him."

My skin heats up. I *hate* that a lot. The fact that he gets to dictate everyone's lives to such an extent is so manipulative. He may not alter my thoughts, or change time to revoke his previous decisions, but he should at least be able to aptly plan. Because he doesn't have a mate, he believes he can play around with the relationships of others.

I hate him for it.

"I'm sure fate didn't decide that I would be going anywhere with you," I exclaim confidently, taking another step backward, hoping he won't notice.

48

Kaden smiles again. It always scares me when he does that. "Perhaps you don't have a very clear judgement."

My jaw clenches.

"Don't you worry, you have a day to make a run for it," he says. "My favorite game is one of chase. It would be boring to just take you right now. Plus, I get to see if you have the guts to confront your mate about this."

This is his challenge. If I don't take it, then I'm sure he would snatch me up right now, and I wouldn't be able to fight back. Lucy can't save me from a court trial, or from years of slavery behind the walls of the vengeance pack. I'm glad she managed to get away, otherwise-

Lucy is suddenly dragged back into the camp area.

A stab of betrayal wedges its way into my stomach, and I don't know why. The strange man from weeks ago who had saved me from being raped was holding my sister. He didn't look friendly anymore, but cold and detached, like his leader.

I should have seen it coming. I shouldn't have trusted him, no matter what he had done for me.

"There are many things you are willing to protect," Kaden says. "I'll be back tomorrow. Do me a favor and at least *try* to entertain me."

He takes a few steps back, and I notice his subtle wink.

"Think about it."

And then he was gone.

Chapter Nine

Dawn

For the first time in a long time, I was stunned speechless.

Kaden and Kace left as swiftly as they had come, leaving Lucy and me confused beyond belief. His words of warning took a few moments to fully develop in my mind as I sank down to sit on the log. He wants me dead. Either that, or he wants me locked away forever in his pack filled with sickening murderers.

Real murderers.

"I don't think we have a choice," I hear Lucy say from behind me. I hated that I had trusted Kace. It had been a detailed game for Kaden since that night two weeks ago.

What has Kaden been doing since? Hanging around the purity pack watching me or terrorizing the innocent members of this pack?

"We aren't going," I growl, knowing what my sister wants.

It wouldn't be giving Rylan the satisfaction, he doesn't care about that. It would be surrendering, and as much as that seems tempting, it's not what I want. If I were to walk into Rylan's territory, it wouldn't be for him. If I were to do so, I would be adamant on not being converted, nor tamed down into a 'perfect' luna.

I wouldn't be tempted by him....

"How else are we going to have any chance to get away from Kaden?" Lucy questions, moving to sit beside me. "He's the alpha of vengeance. Even if you weren't sick, we wouldn't be able to get away from him in a day."

Sighing, I run my hands back through my hair, trying to find a way to distract myself from the situation.

"You know that's what Kaden wants right? For us to go flocking to Rylan."

Shaking her head, Lucy is on her feet again. When she gets flustered in an argument, she can't keep still. The poor girl can't stop her hands trembling, as she tries to win me over. Her change of tact surprises me, but I know she is afraid. Who wouldn't be afraid of the alpha of vengeance? I know I am. But Rylan isn't her mate; she doesn't know what he's like.

"He wants you dead."

"It doesn't matter what he wants. Even if I do get caught, it's the discipline pack jury that decides."

She growls. "And what makes you think they would listen to a desire pack member? How do you know Kaden wouldn't coerce them into sending you to his pack, where some might say you belong?"

"Don't know you know what Rylan will do? He's been killing people just to find me, Lucy. Something clicked in his head that no ten year old should ever have to deal with."

Lucy crosses her arms over her chest in defiance. I probably shouldn't have mentioned her age. "You know I'm eleven soon, right?"

I stand also, grabbing her shoulders. She looks too mature, as the shadows of the increasing night wrap around her shoulders, inching up to her face. There is so much life there that I refuse to let it go to waste. She is too special to me, and as much as our parents hated that about her, I don't.

"I don't want Rylan to change you," I say hoarsely. Thinking about my sister being affected hurts me deep inside.

"He won't.... Please, Dawn."

51

Something in her eyes speaks to me. I know my sister. Now though, I can't tell if she truly wants this life with Rylan, or if she wants me to be safe, and rid of my sickness. With the latter, I'm flattered. However, if she truly wants a life with him, then that changes everything.

"And think, we can easily escape Rylan," Lucy reminds me, holding my hands that were on her shoulders. "We did it once, who is to say we can't do it again."

It was almost too easy to get away from Rylan. He didn't resist.... No one did.

"Plus, great food," Lucy adds.

My jaw clenches. The cool of the night is beginning to attack my skin, lighting it up in shivers. We have little time left to discuss this. If I were to ignore everything my sister was saying to force her to make a break for it toward the freedom pack, we wouldn't make it very far. Darkness is dangerous, no matter where you are within the pack quarter.

"You're sure?" I question uneasily.

She nods. "Positive. I don't think I ever want to see Alpha Kaden's eyes ever again."

At least I can agree with her on that one. His eyes are soulless. It only makes me wonder if he has turned his mate into something as bad as him.

"If I change my mind, we are leaving straight away."

***

His house is terrifying.

The last time I was here, I didn't take the time to truly assess the place. The beauty of it had been absorbed by the night, but right now I could take in the staggering grandeur in front of me. It's old, and it's impressive, and it is something that is so terrifying that it makes me want to turn around and run back the way I came.

It hadn't been hard to get past any guards patrolling the property. Most are out looking for me, and since it's the middle of the day, no one was really there to see us make our way over the wall. Had there not been a tree there, we wouldn't have had a chance to get over.

"We can still go," I remind Lucy, but she furrows her brows and shakes her head at me.

Honestly, I'm scared. Not of Kaden right now. No, of Rylan. Seeing those eyes again seems like such a daunting concept. When I'm around him, I'm afraid everything I have built up against him will be torn down until I am left with no facade left to save me.

Lucy pushes my hand toward the building. If his estate wasn't so magnificent, this may have been less frightening. This place breathes its prosperity and wealth into me, making me feel so insignificant compared to it. It makes me straighten my back, before fearlessly marching toward the main door.

"Do I just knock?"

I almost feel Lucy roll her eyes without even having to look at her.

Slowly, I raise my fist to the door. It takes a few deep breaths and a growl of irritation from Lucy before I actually feel contact between my fingers and the wood. As soon as I draw my hand away, there is a pregnant silence, as we both stare the door down, waiting for whatever may be on the other side of it.

When it opens, I first see the stony face of one of Rylan's personal guards. He stares at me, and I see the flash of disbelief streak through his eyes.

The male has probably been a part of this hunt for me for the past year or so, and probably hates me more than anything for it. So, to see me standing on the doorstep must have shocked him for a moment. Then he takes a step forward toward me, hand ready to grab the thick whip attached to his hip.

Instantly, I move Lucy behind me, holding my free hand up as a silent way to beg for mercy.

"Please, we aren't here to run," I tell him in a rush of words that might not be completely coherent. The guard wants to come at me, to capture me and finally stop this once and for all.

53

"What's going on?"

His voice makes me quiver. The sound of it melts over me, having a calming effect on my body almost instantly. Only one male can make me feel this way...

"It's your mate," the guard says quickly over his shoulder. "It's Dawn."

Rylan was at the door instantly, his eyes wide in disbelief, as he drank in the sight of me on the doorstep. It's hard to function properly when he's looking at me, or when I look at him. He looks as sickly as me, with dark shadows under his eyes that contrasted against pasty skin. He's feeling this as much as I am.

Or maybe it's the guilt of what he has done to try to get me here.

There is only a split second where he takes a moment to register for things. Then, he is moving toward me, before I put my hands up, warning him not to come closer.

"I'm not going to run," I say shakily, the silvery blue of his eyes pinning me down. "Just please, not any closer."

He listens, not taking another step through the door. Before I can let him come anywhere near me - let alone touch me - I have to assert the rules, otherwise Rylan is going to whisk me away in the mate bond, and I can't have that. Just looking in his eyes is enough to weaken me at the knees, however, I am careful to keep my ground.

"I have so many questions," Rylan murmurs.

Taking a deep breath, I slowly pull Lucy out from behind me. Rylan instantly frowns, before a flash of recognition for the young girl crosses his features. Lucy and I look very alike, so it isn't hard for him to figure it out.

Lucy stays frozen as I look straight up at Rylan. "Can we come in?"

His mouth parts slightly in shock, obviously not expecting me to say that. Instead of throwing more questions my way, he steps back so Lucy and I can walk in through the front door.

54

I'm instantly enveloped in his familiar, calming scent. It makes me relax involuntarily, but Lucy clinging to me is a painful reminder of why I am here. To protect her, and myself, from the megalomaniac Alpha Kaden.

The door suddenly slams behind us. There's no escape now.

Chapter Ten

Dawn

I shudder at the sight of the closed door. It's a symbol of finality.

If I had tried to get Lucy to stop cutting the circulation off in my hand, I would have had to pry her fingers off with some vicious tool. She hates the idea of being trapped as much as I do, and not knowing what is in our futures is yet another daunting thought.

Rylan regards us silently, waiting for the right moment to bring up the questions he is so desperately wanting to berate us with. He knows he is walking on eggshells.

"You don't have to explain," Rylan says smoothly. I can tell that's his way of making me feel comfortable, yet I can still see in his eyes that he's fighting his curiosity. I don't blame him. I'm sure the last thing he would expect from me is to show up at his door after this entire pursuit thing we've had going.

I exhale slowly. "Kaden wants me dead."

Rylan closes his eyes. He knew the weight of the situation the moment I mentioned his name. For many years, Rylan had been trying to avoid Kaden's wrath to keep his pack safe. Now, someone who is supposed to be their luna has lead them straight to him, and into his line of fire.

"Because of the guard?"

I nod.

Guilt seeps into the back of my mind, but I do my best to dismiss it. What I did was an accident, yet for some reason, that's hard to swallow.

"What did he say to you?" Rylan questions, his shoulders growing tense, his eyes darkening with every word. I can't tell if it's his instinct as an alpha that is kicking in, or the mate bond. Whatever it is, it's a frightening look on him.

"He was being deceptive and odd," I tell him, remembering his words.

There was no part of our conversation where I felt like I knew what exactly Kaden wanted. At the same time as wanting me dead, or living as a slave in his pack, he wants me to protect myself. Either he's sick in the head, or maybe there is something else to it. If he is as manipulative as people say he is, then I can't be sure.

"Typical," Rylan mutters sardonically. Then he focuses his full attention back to me. "Thank you for coming to me."

I shrug and a blanket of silence falls over us.

"Someone can take your sister to get cleaned up, if you're both okay with that," Rylan suggests gently, nodding to someone behind us.

When I turn, I see an older looking woman with a cautious smile wander closer. If she wasn't someone who worked for Rylan, I would have thought her to be someone I would typically get along with. However, in this situation, I can't tell what her motive is. Lucy flinches as the lady touches her arm.

I give Rylan a suspicious look and he sighs. "I promise you won't be separated for long. And she won't hurt her...."

If anyone could look after themselves well, it's Lucy. Just from looking at the woman, I couldn't help but trust her just a little bit. Being a true born purity pack member, from the looks of it, she shouldn't want to hurt anyone. Especially not an innocent ten-year-old girl. Not that she could anyway, since Lucy doesn't go down without a fight.

"I'm not worried about Lucy," I say carefully. "I'm worried about your member getting hurt."

57

Rylan didn't doubt it. He saw what Lucy did to get me back, and he would be stupid not to think she would do it again. Even I'm a little worried she'll lash out after being confined in this place, despite how large it is.

However, she takes me by surprise by taking the woman's hand while letting mine go.

She's smart enough to know I have to deal with this before it manifests into something worse. Rylan may be the only way to keep us safe, and even though my entire body is quivering, wanting to flee, for Lucy's safety, I'm going to stay with this alpha and hope the mate bond between us will stay calm enough for my head to keep clear.

I watch her walk off, trying to avoid eye contact with Rylan. That's the way he sucks me in like a hypnotist.

"I've been worried about you," Rylan murmurs. "Really worried."

For whatever reason, I had expected him to be mad at me, wanting me restrained after my escape in the restaurant. Every time I think about it, I remember the look in his eyes. I hate the way it hurts me. Even looking at him now, the fact I can see he is clearly unwell has me on edge for him, even if I probably look twice as bad.

I look down at my fingers. "You didn't have to be. You know I belong beyond on the wall... Lucy and I both."

"I know. You're safer here, though," he says. He's right.

Kaden would have to drag an entire army into this pack in order to find a way in. That thought alone drapes a security blanket over my shoulders. What if Rylan wasn't my mate? Kaden's ultimatum wouldn't exist, and I would be in a holding cell in the discipline pack by now.

"Thank you, by the way," I offer, bringing my gaze up so he can see how sincere I was being. There may be a cold drift between us, but at the very least, I can respect him for that much.

"You don't have to thank me," he adds. "I'll do anything for you. Don't you know that?"

He takes a deep breath and comes towards me, reaching out. I match it back.

There is a lot I can handle, but his touch isn't included in that. The spark felt between mates is something that cannot be simply translated into anything else. It's unique, and that's distracting. The last thing I need to be doing right now is getting distracted by Rylan. The heady mix of his touch and presence might be enough to undo me in my current state.

I'm stronger than that.

"I can understand why you're worried, Rylan, but I'll be fine," I tell him securely, straightening my shoulders as if to prove my point. The action makes me hurt my neck a little. Either that or this dizzying feeling is from my weakness.

My eyes almost cross as my vision blurs, and for a moment, I question whether or not I'm going to remain conscious, or if I'm going to topple to the floor. In less than a second, Rylan is steadying me, his hands firmly holding my biceps as I try find my balance.

"I knew it," Rylan mutters distastefully while I gather my wits. "You're seriously not well."

"I'll be fine," I mutter, sounding almost drunk. However, my hands find the broad expanse of his shoulders, absently gripping onto the hard muscle under his shirt to keep myself up.

Just his scent of cashmere, wood and citrus has my mind spinning.

I didn't really have much time to protest, as Rylan stepped forward to wrap his arms around me, picking me up as if I were some kind of blushing bride. My scowl of irritation is smothered by a jolt of pain to my head, similar to what I felt when I was being pursued by the elites. This time, though, Rylan is here to catch me, even if it's going against what I wanted from the start.

He carries me upstairs, with each step feeling like a punch to my nose. My forehead is jarring with pain. I keep my head close to Rylan's chest, feeling the warmth through his shirt and hearing the sound of his beating heart.

"This is why I tried so hard to find you," Rylan mutters, and I'm not sure if he was speaking to me or himself.

All of a sudden, I'm back in the room again. It's the same room I had previously been in when I was first taken here. When I had escaped, I had safely assumed I would never have to see it ever again. However, this time, I'm not as terrified of it as I was. This time, I welcome the silken sheets under my skin as Rylan sets me down gently.

For the first time in a long time, my body relaxes and the dizzying colors spanning across my vision cease.

"I haven't been eating," I admit. I don't want him to assume it's because of our lack of proximity. "That's all."

He shakes his head, looking like a disapproving parent for a moment. I can see the way it distresses him with the look in his eyes. Without even realizing it, he can be very expressive with his eyes, laying out an entire selection of his feelings, which can sometimes be hard to handle. It hits me square in the heart.

As I feel myself coming back to my normal self, I sit up, clutching my head as if it might make a difference to my sanity. Thankfully, my mind manages to stay stable.

He sits beside me, and I wonder if he would leave me if I asked him to. I can't bring myself to do so.

"I'm sorry for everything I've done to find you," Rylan murmurs. "I hate myself for it, but you drove me crazy day and night."

I keep my mouth shut, trying not to mention the amount of times I looked up into the sky, wondering where Rylan was, and what he was doing. As much as I try my best to avoid mentioning it, I do think about him. It's like some strange compulsion that I want to act on, but I have to restrain myself when it comes to walking straight through his door and back into his arms again....

Until now, of course.

"We are just as bad as each other," I note, shrugging slightly.

Really, we aren't. I'm a desire pack member who shouldn't care about their actions. He is the alpha of the purest pack in the quarter, who has a reputation to uphold.

"They fear me now. My own pack fears me," Rylan says. I can see the way he's going over all his regrets in his eyes.

I shock myself by grabbing his hand.

The spark is there, naturally. The feeling begins from my fingertips, streaming up my arms before it consumes my entire being. Instantly, I could feel myself heal from the inside, that simple spark between us reaching into my heart to give me a moment of bliss through all the pain and weakness I've felt during these past few days.

"You're an alpha. Isn't that the point?" I question, almost sounding slightly breathless.

He smiles, not letting my hand go. His grip is as sturdy as a walking stick underneath me, keeping me able to sit up properly.

"Perhaps," he says softly. "Perhaps being an alpha makes me a terrible person."

My mind comes back to Kaden. Not that I have ever met any other alphas than Rylan and Kaden, but I believe I can safely assume all alphas are different from your average pack member.

And as much as Rylan may hate to admit it, he may just be as forbidding as all of them.

Chapter Eleven

Dawn

That night, I dreamt of when Rylan and I first met.

"It's our only choice," I hear her murmur. I keep my head behind the wall, trying my best not to be tempted to look around the corner.

My father sighs. "She won't like it. *They* won't like it."

My nails dig into the wall. I know what they're talking about. It's only been a week since we first arrived in the purity pack, and they are already talking about shipping Lucy and I off to some boarding school at the end of the pack. It makes me ill just thinking of being locked up in school, just to pray to a goddess I don't believe in.

"It doesn't matter what they like or not," says my mother insistently. "They come from the desire pack. They need to be raised properly from now on. They need to be put in their place."

My teeth grind against each other as I continue to clench my jaw. It was *her* idea to bring us here in the first place.

"Dawn will get mad, but she will get over it. Lucy is only nine, she won't be hard to convince," she adds. I can imagine her close to Father, trying to convince him with only her dark brooding eyes that this is actually okay. That she can take his children away from him.

I decide to be brave enough to lean out enough to view the conversation.

My father is pressed back against the counter, my mother in front of him. For someone so convinced that the moon goddess is someone we need to respect, she is acting awfully like a desire pack member. That's who we are. I don't know why she is so set on changing that fact.

"Dawn will hate us. You know she gets anxiety about being locked in one place for too long. She's different," Father tries to reason.

Stop while you can. I've tried to explain.

"Different won't cut it!"

I flinched back behind the wall at her yell. Those same eyes, which I inherited from her, are blazed with a hot poker into my mind. She is still the same. Does she seriously think moving to a pack of virtue and religion is going to turn her anger off automatically like a switch? I've heard enough....

I've been planning this since I was first told we were moving from the desire pack to the purity pack. I'm going to take my sister, and we will escape. My plan isn't perfect, but we don't have much time. I won't feel safe until we are on the other side of this pack's walls and away from any risk of a boarding school.

I find her in her bed. Before waking her, I pack us some spare belongings in a backpack. She doesn't protest when I whisper what I've heard in her ear and relay what my plan is.

She's too smart for that.

Disappearing into the night was the easy part. We lived close to the border, and the shadows gave good enough shelter for us. Alpha Rylan doesn't worry much about security around these parts ... or in fact, around any parts.

I had just hoisted Lucy up the wall when it happened. I had underestimated him, and it came back to bite me in the ass.

As a line of guards emerged from the shadows of the marketplace, Lucy had just managed to conceal herself. It was me against them. I saw them brandishing their weapons. It may have

63

been only three of them, but it was enough for me to know that I stood no real chance of escaping.

They didn't have to ask for an excuse from me. They simply slapped some handcuffs on my wrists and dragged me from the square.

"Why waste his time?" I hear one of the guards utter as we walk down the cobblestone street, my feet stumbling along with them. I'm yet to find out where I'm going to be taken. I assume I will be questioned by a law enforcer who will find my parents and force them to take me straight to the boarding school before I can attempt to run away.

All the while, Lucy is still out there.

"It's about time he sees how much some people hate this pack," another guard replies. He leans down over me, pulling back my veil of dark hair that I had been hiding behind.

"Where you from?" he questions. I glare back into his cruel eyes. "Vengeance? Desire?"

I growl in response.

"He's the alpha. He doesn't have any interest in a young female trying to escape," the more sensible guard muses. This guy pulling on my hair, dragging me by my arm, should really take some advice from the others.

"Come on, he's just got back from his run," the guard holding me taunts. "Let's humor him."

The alpha runs at night?

I was dragged down a few more streets, the pushing and the shoving never ceasing, despite my willingness to comply. If I'm not let off now, I'll be sent straight to the school, and all my chances of ever escaping and finding Lucy again will disappear. I've never met an Alpha, but that doesn't mean I won't be able to talk my way into innocence. He's the alpha of purity after all.

Well, here's hoping, I suppose.

The alpha had in fact been on a night run in wolf form. He emerged from a small group of his guards that were protecting a tight corridor that must lead to the outside. His own personal runway to escape. Wish I had one too.

Clearly he had just shifted, otherwise you would never catch the alpha of purity without his shirt on around anyone else. Luckily, he enough time to put pants on.

I didn't pay much attention to his body, or at least, I tried my best not to. His eyes were what captured me.

He seemed surprised at my presence. I don't blame him. Why should an alpha have to deal with an unruly girl trying to run away? The guards were probably looking to shame me in front of him so I would back to my mother crying. One day I'll be strong enough to retaliate against them.

When I escape, I'll come back for them

He stares at me, eyebrows furrowed. The darkness drifts around him, masking his face, accentuating the sharpness of his jawline and cheekbones. I could see the alpha in him; an average male doesn't carry himself like that. He's clearly the embodiment of all that he stands for, and it's instantly intimidating.

"What is this?" he questions, his voice thick and pure with an accent only derived from this pack.

I want to cower away. If there is anyone who I can get in the biggest trouble with, it's an alpha. Especially the one of the pack I just tried to make an escape from.

"Thought you might want to deal with this one," the guard holding me says with a guttural laugh. He shoves me forward, until I stumble onto the ground, my knees hitting the hard concrete under me. I bit back a groan of complaint. Okay, that hurt my pride more than it hurt my body.

Rylan narrows his eyes at the guard, offering me a hand until I was pulled back up by the collar of my shirt. Back into the arms of the guard I go.

"You know what happens to my guards who play around with innocent girls?" he asks, his voice deviously soft.

65

"Trust me, she ain't innocent," the guard mutters, pulling my hair back until I'm forced to move my face back, exposing half my face to the pig. "Caught her trying to escape over the main wall."

I could see Rylan watching me carefully. He didn't move though.

"Then she is the business of the lower guards. They will send her back to her family," Rylan says gruffly.

He went to turn away. At that moment, I could have been taken away, and he would have never found out. He had been done with me - a lowly, delinquent girl. Rylan would have gone back to being an alpha, and I would have never crossed his mind ever again. The way he turned his back on me showed me clearly that he was discarding me.

The guard just *had* to say something.

"Don't you want to deal with this before we send her back? That way she can go crying to all the others there and scare them all off from ever wanting to escape this pack," the guard says.

Rylan paused, dark hair moving with him as he turned his head slightly. He didn't once look at me as he gave the guard his full attention again. I kept quiet, just in case.

"And how do you suggest I punish her, guard?" he questioned.

A wolfish grin covered his expression. "However you please, Alpha."

Then his gaze was on mine. It was direct, undeviating. There is something so unbelievably unique about the silvery blue color that drew me in.

"Why don't you come here and I'll show these guards that we treat people well in this pack," Rylan says, a warmth to his tone that is almost too attractive.

Before I could move myself, I was ruthlessly shoved forward.

And that was how we touched.

His hands came out to grab mine, wrapping around my fingers. It was almost like an electrical outlet plugging in, as a multitude of undeniable sparks coursed through my fingers to the rest of my

66

body. It gave me such a fright, I jumped back, but he was quick to remain hold of me.

"No," I say quickly as waves of emotions crashed over me. "No, this can't be."

I tried to push him back, but he moved to hold my shoulder securely. His face had confusion written all over it as he looked down at me, clearly trying to figure out how this could have happened. He may even have wondered why the moon goddess would have been cruel enough to do this to him.

"It's okay." He breathed, perhaps to soothe me as I continued to struggle against him.

Then I was ripped from his grip by an unknowing guard. Instantly, I watched as Rylan's expression darkened, his jaw ticking as anger crawled across his features.

"Let her go," he muttered.

"Sorry about her, Alpha," the guard said, clearly not knowing what had just transpired between us. "We will send her to the lower guards."

"No," he growled, and the guard was quick to let me go. "That's my mate you were just touching."

At that moment, my mind was too clouded to think straight. Fathoming the fact that I had just found my mate, and that he was an alpha, was impossible. It wasn't even my mind's choice as I darted to the left, slipping from all their surprised gasps as I made a run for it. It didn't take much to escape them. I had the element of surprise, and the shadows played into my favor.

From then, I wandered into the forest and began my new life.

Gasping awake, I clung to the first thing there, with its arms around me.

Rylan.

Chapter Twelve

Dawn

"Let's make a deal," I say firmly, planting my hands on the table in front of him.

Rylan looks up at me in surprise, he's clearly not expecting me to come down here at this time of night. The last time I saw him, we had been sitting on the bed talking about how he may not be a very good alpha. Moments later, I must have fallen into slumber, since I can't remember a thing after that. Well, aside from the dream.

His silvery blue eyes glint in the lamp light. "A deal?"

"Yes." I breathe. "A deal."

His mouth twists slightly as he mulls over my words, then he motions over to the seat in front of him, careful not to spill the dark liquid in his glass. I take a moment before I back up, sinking into the seat without taking my eyes off his.

"You should be in bed," he says, raising a dark eyebrow. I shrug carelessly, trying to act as if crawling out of bed at midnight to find him wasn't difficult.

I'm still sick, however, I won't let him have the pleasure of knowing that.

"I'm fine," I tell him carefully.

He takes a sip of his drink, and I wonder what it is. Alcohol? I didn't think purity pack members were allowed to indulge in something that might tempt them into doing something... sinful. I don't ask him though, as he sits forward. "You're not fine."

"You don't know me," I respond firmly.

"You act as though you aren't sitting in front of your mate right now," he comments, throwing back the rest of the drink before sliding the glass onto the table in front of me. Whatever is in that cup, it doesn't seem to faze him.

I grind my teeth together to keep myself calm. "That's what this deal is all about. If it can really be classified as one."

Rylan's eyes narrow. He's an alpha who knows what he wants, and it will take a lot to sway him. There is no way he is going to agree to the idea I came up with when I first woke up. We are both as stubborn as each other, so I can assume there will be a lot of arguing in our future.

"Humor me, Dawn."

"I'm going to summon Fate, and he's going to change who my mate is," I say confidently.

Rylan is on his feet in a second. For the alpha of purity, I would have expected a fleeting moment of anger, before he righted himself and went over what I was proposing. However, Rylan picked up his empty glass, sized it up for a moment and threw it over my head, where it smashed against the wall behind me.

I gasp, turning around to see the glass shatter and fall to the ground in a mass of glistening crystal. When I twist back around, Rylan has his back to me, his hands dug deep into his hair.

"What happened to you?" I question breathlessly.

I'm not looking at my mate. I'm looking at a changed man. I stand abruptly when he doesn't answer. "Was it Kaden? Did he turn you into this?"

"No, Dawn," he muttered gruffly, turning around so I get a glimpse of the feral look in his eyes. "*You* did this to me."

I flinch, taking a few steps back. When I ran away for the year, I thought I'd had it worse off. I had no idea that I would turn Rylan into someone completely unrecognizable. Does his pack know

69

about this? Of course they do; he's been terrorising them to get to me. A gargantuan amount of guilt I've been trying to fight off settles on my shoulders.

"That's exactly why I'm going to summon Fate," I tell him securely, straightening my shoulders so I don't seem intimidated by his sudden change in attitude.

He shakes his head at me, eyes darkening. "Not happening."

"This is my decision. I'll make a deal with him, I'll do anything... anything for a new mate," I say slowly.

Rylan sighs, before he starts taking small, taunting steps toward me. I found myself scrambling back until my back was pressed against the wall; the hard wood keeping grounded to the situation. The look in his eyes is something I would describe as typically alpha. Not just any alpha, though. An alpha of vengeance, perhaps?

"You know you belong to me, right?" he questions, his head tilting in a crazed way. I'm tempted to slap him, as if it would bring some sense into him.

"As if," I growl. "God, what happened to you? You're a different person."

Rylan's hands move to either side of my head; they press against the wood so hard I hear it creak. I can still see the same male there, except he is hiding behind a veil that he's been forced to bring up after I left.

"That's what happens when your mate runs away from you, as if you're some kind of disease," he mutters. "How have you not gone into your heat yet? Being away from me does more to you than make you a little weak."

"I'm fully aware of that, Alpha, but stronger than you think," I growl.

Rylan brings his fingers up. I watch them nervously as he brings them close my face, tracing my jawline without even touching me. "I'm not doubting how strong you are. But I'm still surprised."

Then he touches me. The tip of his index finger brushes the skin of my cheek, and my back instinctively arches off the wall. I see

70

enjoyment, the victory that dances in his eyes. He knows how the sparks control me and how my body bows to them without any authority. They are the one thing I have been trying to avoid.

"Kiss me," I snap, the unyielding tone in my voice starting to waver. "You think you have so much control over me? Then show me how the alpha of purity can resist his mate."

He growls. This is my playing card. When he first dragged me in I managed to figure out that he'd still clung to his morals, not wanting to get dragged away from his religion. I'm pressing him so I can figure out why exactly he doesn't want any intimacy.

I'm not complaining ... I'm just curious.

His thumb comes up to my lip, brushing it slightly. I see where his gaze is directed. He's not fooling me. However, he resists, clenching his jaw tightly as if a slip of a single word would send him over the edge.

"What is it? You have to marry me before you can touch me?" I question, a slight smile tugging away at my lips. "Remind me, since I'm not really a part of your pack."

Rylan sighS deeply in an act of irritation. "There's a ceremony. It happens on the full moon in the month of June, when the moon goddess supposedly looks down to witness and grant permission to mates. Everybody waits until this time to mark their mates. Part of my religion states I can't ... be with you until that night."

I take a deep breath, completely understanding his words. "That's a month from now."

"Stop. Tempting. Me."

I push at his chest, ducking under his outstretched arms while tucking my own around my chest. It all made sense now. His foolish belief in the moon goddess has gotten him to this point. Almost everyone knows she backed down from her power. She doesn't decide things anymore. The megalomaniac Fate does.

I'm not going to bother explaining it to Rylan, though. His entire pack worships the goddess.

71

"Listen," I say softly, turning back around to face him. "I'm going to see Fate, and I'm going to change the mate bond."

He shakes his head me. "Even if I let you, how can you be sure it's even possible?"

Fate is a cruel man; at least that's what I've heard. However, he is willing to strike a deal with whoever may present one. I'm sure if I can bargain something, he will take away the mate bond and give Rylan a better mate. Someone who lost theirs to death and deserves someone as sweet and kind as the alpha. Someone who doesn't mind living under all his rules.

"Positive."

Rylan leans back against the wall, watching me with a brooding expression on his face. Clearly, he's thinking this over. Thinking of a way to keep me from breaking another one of his rules.

"All right, you want a deal, we can make a deal," he says suddenly. My eyebrows quirk up in surprise. This is unexpected.

"Go on."

"Give me a month to prove to you that I can be the mate you want," he says slowly, almost as if I wouldn't catch it. "You can make your decision on the night of the moon ceremony. If you want to be with me, I'll mark you. If not, you can go to Fate."

I narrow my eyes at him. "Okay, I like that. One thing though..."

He nods at me to continue.

"My sister can leave whenever she pleases. You will not require her to believe in anything about your special little goddess, and you will not send her away to any boarding facility. This is between you and me, and you will not use her at all to get to me," I say, laying my rules out before him.

"I thought a lot of that was a given," he notes, then shrugs. "All right, I can agree to that. Your sister will have nothing to do with this deal, unless of course, you say so."

A weight was lifted off my chest at that. I *had* to make sure she was safe.

"Anything on your part?" I ask.

"All I ask for is to you to at least try," he says gently. "Just a little."

Sighing deeply, I nod. "Okay, deal."

Rylan smiles, but it doesn't reach his eyes. He looks grim, and something tells me it has to do with him nearly losing it when I mentioned Fate. He doesn't think I'm willing to figure out how he turned into that.

He grabs my hand, and gently kisses it.

"Let the fun begin. Am I right?"

Chapter Thirteen

Dawn

"I'm fine, Dawny. I understand why you want to do this."

I gaze down at my young sister, who is all dressed up and looking pretty. She suits this lifestyle, I have decided, and I'm going to make sure she finds someone who will take care of her and let her do as she pleases. Her mate, or not.

"Rylan even came to see me," she adds, hoping off her bed to wander off to her vanity. It's strange how this all belongs to her now. "He said I can go anywhere on his property. Even inside the gardens."

"It doesn't bother you that you can't go outside anymore? Into the forest, I mean?"

Lucy shakes her head at me, picking the hairbrush up to run it through her hair. Had she been lying to me when she told me she loved the freedom over a conventional lifestyle? Her beauty at least will help her fit in here. Those doe eyes and that button nose. She is only young, but I can already see her being extremely successful in life.

"It's new, and I like that. It's only early days yet, but I might even consider going to school here or something," she adds, smiling brightly into the mirror.

The novelty will wear off, Lucy.

I keep my mouth shut. I'm not going to mention her sudden change of tact or address my distaste for her words. It's her choice what she decides to do with her life, not mine. However, it makes me nervous to think how easily influenced she may be by other purity pack members.

"Anyways, don't you and Rylan have a date today, or something?" she questions, standing back up again to wander over to me.

Ah yes. I'm surprised he wants to get into this straight away, considering the whole mating ceremony is a whole month away. If anything, I thought I would be locked away in my room, yet he is actually letting me out after what happened. I can imagine the security when we leave this place, he'll probably be keeping me prisoner, even out in public.

"Something like that." I breathe.

She places her hands on her shoulders and smiles at me. "I think I'm going to play around in the garden or something."

Good. Be a kid, for once.

Lucy leaves in a flurry of white fabric and dark hair. It strikes me as more than strange that she's changed her mind about living here so quickly. Back in the forest, she would trash-talk Rylan more than I would.

Shaking my head in wonder, I follow her out the door, however, I walk the opposite way. I've agreed to try with Rylan, which means going along with his little date idea. In reality, I want to stress my rules of freedom around here... maybe even convince him to let me out of here for a few hours on the terms that, of course, I would come back.

Maybe. I'm feeling better now that I'm eating properly again.

The moment I turn the corner to walk down the stairs, I'm brought to a startled stop. A man stands at the top of the stairs, leaning against the banister; a brooding expression on his face.

He stands tall at the sight of me, an immediate grin dancing across his lips. I'm taken aback by him, and the way he looks. I've never seen someone with hair that is such a luminous dark blue. It's scattered across the man's forehead, going down to his eyes; which are a threatening obsidian color.

75

He skips forward on light steps and holds his hand out to me. "Good morning, Dawn. Wow, this must be your favorite time of day."

I'm not sure if I'm struggling to react to the lame joke or just by him in general.

"You work for Rylan," I decide. Why else would he be here?

He frowns, then chuckles animatedly. The way he laughs is interesting, as if it has been locked away for quite some time, and doesn't see the sun very often.

"I don't work for anyone, honey," he says, sobering from his laugh. "I'm Fate."

My surprise knocks me still for a moment. Fate? Now I suddenly see it, why he looks so strange and doesn't seem to belong anywhere within the pack quarter. My mind still scrambles for reason behind his sudden appearance, which I assume is because of Rylan. Or maybe it has something to do with my threats to find him and get him to revoke our meeting bond.

Finally, Fate retracts his hand, tucking it behind his back. He balances the tips of his shoes to the heel, before glancing over his shoulder. Seeming irritated by what he saw, he suddenly grabbed my hand and walked me toward the nearest door, shouldering it open, before leading me into the small office-like area.

"We have something important to discuss," he says, letting go of my arm as he shuts the door behind us.

I fold my arms over my chest, watching him wander over to the desk in the middle of the room. Without a care for any property damage, he sits squarely on the desk. Luckily, there are no papers or anything for him to accidentally ruin.

"Do we?" I ask in disbelief. If anything, I would expect him to take Rylan up with any issues he has, not me. Especially since I haven't been living here for more than a day.

"You have every right to be angry at me," he says, although I can tell he doesn't care really care if I do or don't. He has that kind of tone about him, as if nothing can touch him. If what I have

76

learned about Fate throughout the years is true, then that can be justified. He is completely untouchable.

"Why?" I question warily.

Fate sighs deeply, and for a moment, he looks troubled. "I convinced your sister it's okay to be here. That she doesn't need to be out there."

My eyes widen in shock as his words sink in. What does he mean by *convinced*? My sister does not simply get convinced, especially by someone like Fate. She surely would have mentioned seeing him. It all leads me to believe…

"Okay, I messed with her head a little bit, but it's all in good will," Fate says carefully, his eyes narrowing slightly, as if he was wishing he were telling me something else.

Anger suddenly consumes every pore in my body. You don't mess with my sister,

"Messed with her? If you weren't omnipotent or whatever, I would kill you right now," I mutter darkly, my eyes landing on his neck. I'd heard he was manipulative and does whatever he can to get what he wants, but this is something I never saw coming. My sister means too much to me. "Tell me what you-"

Fate holds his hands up. "Calm down. She attacked one of Rylan's staff, so I calmed her down and used a little... incentive, to help her understand what is going on, and what is going happen."

"Why?" I question, unable to keep my rapid breathing in check. "Why help her, if that's even what you're doing?"

Then the smile was back.

"I need your help, and I believe you need mine."

Instantly, I shake my head. I've learned enough about him to know not to make a deal with him. I may come from the desire pack where we worship Fate - the only immortal who will let everyone get away with their sins - however, there isn't a single person in their right mind who isn't wary of him.

"I don't need anything from you. Fix my sister, and leave," I snap, glad that my voice isn't trembling. Wherever this confidence has come from, I want more of it.

He shakes his head in wonder. "Don't you need someone on your side? You have an alpha who wants you dead, and another who wants you locked up to be his pretty little princess. It doesn't look like you have many other options."

"Rylan and I are compromising," I say carefully.

"That doesn't change Kaden, does it?" Fate says, still smiling as if enjoying a personal joke. "He isn't going to stop until you're dead. Usually, he wouldn't be so *involved* since his daughter was born a month ago. However, you're different."

I knew what he was going to say…

"You're Rylan's mate, and the fact that he is the alpha of purity and you will be his luna makes you as pure as him. Well, presumably."

At his words, I shiver. At this point, the smile has disappeared, and I can see the seriousness in those endless dark eyes. He isn't worried about me, I know that much. There is something else he wants, otherwise he wouldn't be here.

"Well, thank you for reminding me of my terrible life," I growl, turning my back on him. "I don't want anything from you."

Swinging the door open, I'm startled by the sight of Fate standing right there. Oh yes, another perk of being immortal, I suppose. Placing my hand over my frantically beating heart, I shoulder past him.

He grabs my arm in a tight grip, pulling me back against him. I gasp at our sudden proximity. "I have a friend, and he needs your help."

"Excuse me?"

"There are people like me out there you don't want to meet. Worse than me," he growls in my ear, his breath burning hot. "Some that don't care about immortals like you. So, if you don't want a visit from the man himself, then I suggest you listen."

78

I keep my mouth shut.

"Ever heard of the devil? What about the seven deadly sins?" he questions.

"Myths," I reply.

Fate chuckles. "No, only the nightmares of reality."

I pull my arm away from Fate's grip, rubbing at the spot he'd held me. "I don't see your point. If this is your way of threatening me, then it's pitiful."

"I'm warning you. There is death, but after that, there is something worse. There is purgatory, where a devilish man named Sinful decides your fate. Yes, your fate."

"First," I say slowly. "Sinful is a stupid name. Second, you're Fate, which means you're either really bad at storytelling, or you aren't as powerful as everyone likes to think."

Fate frowns. The expression looks strange on him.

"He wants something, and it looks like you're the perfect way for him to get it," Fate muses, and suddenly, the easy smile I want to slap right off him is making an appearance again. "It does follow his namesake, after all."

"What's that supposed to mean?" I question, although I think I may already know the answer.

"Well, Rylan is the alpha of purity, and Sinful happens to... disagree with a few of his life choices."

"Oh no," I whisper. "He wants me to make Rylan sin."

Chapter Fourteen

Dawn

I find myself chuckling after the words came out of my mouth.

He wants me to make Rylan sin.

"Rylan murdered people," I tell Fate, although he doesn't look convinced. "I heard it myself. Everyone in this pack is terrified of him."

"He never killed those people with his own hands, Dawn," he said tenderly, as if it would rip me open to hear him say that. In actual fact, I found myself beyond confused. I'd heard what people felt about him, and it was terror. "He's an alpha. He gets people to do his dirty work for him."

Of course. "Maybe he indirectly caused the murder, but he still did cause it. It was his idea. I don't know about this strange guy you speak of, but that sounds a lot like one of the biggest sins in the book."

Fate shook his head in the way that makes you feel as if you've just said something beyond stupid.

"That isn't what Sinful wants," Fate tells me slowly. Again, another way of him making me feel incapable of comprehending anything. "What Sinful wants, is Rylan to do something completely forbidden. As his mate, I don't see why you wouldn't be able to do something to sway him away from his beliefs before the ceremony."

80

My eyes widen as I digest his words. Is he being serious? That has to be some form of manipulation I don't want anything to do with.

"Are you saying I need to seduce him, or something?" I question, unable to fully believe it myself.

Fate shrugs, before he brushes past me, moving swiftly down the stairs. Clearly, he has no worry of being seen by anyone, considering how casual he is acting. Is Rylan were to walk in right now, or even one of his staff, I wouldn't know how to explain myself. Only that I was discussing ruining Rylan's reputation as the alpha of purity for someone who is compared to the Devil.

That's one way to get discarded by him.

"I'm saying you might want to do something before Sinful gets involved himself," Fate says sternly, and I sigh deeply. "Don't you think he's tempted by you?"

"You're afraid of him," I say, my expression deadpan.

Fate's jaw clenches as he takes the last step down the stairs. He turns to me.

"I know few people who aren't." Then he disappeared as if he never existed.

***

"Seriously ..." I say, holding my wrists up.

Rylan's hand hovers over the back door handle, a frown etched onto his face as he looks back at me and my awaiting wrists.

He wants to take me outside, and I'm having a hard time believing it. After chasing me down for an entire year, I can't see why he would want to let me out again. Maybe he knows I would make it past his main gate before he shifted and dragged me back inside again for me to brood and disagree with him.

"I think I would rather have handcuffs slapped on me than be tackled by some of your guards," I reason, bringing my arms down after Rylan gives me a clear look that it's not going to happen.

"We're just going out to the garden," he says, popping the door open so I can see the world outside.

From what I could see, there was nowhere for me to be able to run. In fact, the entire backyard is closed off by a large wall I would never have a hope of climbing over. He is going to let me out into a small enclosed space outside with a little bit of sky to see and maybe some flowers if I'm lucky. At least the wall is a little better than ties around my wrist.

"Come on," Rylan prompts softly. "I just want to talk."

Slowly, I slide my hand into his. He wears his gloves again, except this time, they are made out of the softest velvet that soothes my skin as he wraps his fingers around mine. This is his way of keeping his distance until the Moon Ceremony. Fate's words play in my mind.

Don't you think he gets tempted by you?

His garden is kind of an unruly mess, but I don't mind. The moment I step outside, I feel the long grass that goes up to my ankles and the brittle air that shocks some life into my system, I feel all the better. Fate's words float to the back of my mind, and I begin to concentrate on Rylan. His smile is warm as he gazes down at me, watching for a reaction.

"Talk about what, exactly?" I ask distractedly, hardly noticing Rylan closing the door behind me. My skin shivers in anticipation as I look toward where we must be heading.

Rylan's hand squeezes mine a little harder. "Us, I suppose."

The path we stroll down is covered in overgrown grass. Obviously, no one keeps the garden tidy or anything, considering the state of it. Strangely though, it makes me feel at home, like the forest is opening up back around me again, even if they are just ornamental trees and cute flowers that smell sickly sweet.

"What's there to talk about?" I question.

"How this next month is going to go, if you're willing to listen," he says softly, the sound of his voice matching perfectly with the gentle breeze around us. It whispers through the leaves of the garden that we're wandering aimlessly through.

82

It's not much of a garden really. Just patches of dysfunctional plants in completely disarray. I could spend hours in this place, however, I won't yet give Rylan the satisfaction of knowing.

"Can I guess?"

Rylan looks down at me warily. "Okay?"

"You're going to wear your gloves around me at all times. Eye contact is our only form of contact, aside from maybe hand-holding. We won't sleep in the same room, let alone the same bed, and you will try your best to avoid me while I try my best to maybe forgive you for everything you have done in the past."

There are a few moments of silence as we walk. Rylan is probably gathering some kind of response to the truth in my words.

Suddenly, he takes me by surprise.

He turns, grabbing my biceps as he backs me up until I'm pressed against a tree. All the breath is knocked out of me, and not from the impact. In actual fact, my lungs refuse to work as I stare into his silvery eyes, trying to make sense of his actions.

"I'm the alpha of purity." He breathes. "I think I can control myself."

"You weren't saying that previously," I reply, using all the force in my body to not look down at his lips, which are awfully close to mine. Part of me wants to rip away, but the other, lonely part is entranced by his every movement.

He chuckles slightly. "I was teasing you. I wanted a reaction from you, and I clearly got one."

For some reason, that claim made me extremely angry. As his gaze flickered to my lips, I contemplated kneeing him in the stomach. Maybe that would get a *reaction* out of *him,* and I would be the one pinning him to a tree and laughing in his face. However, the more I thought about it, it didn't seem as though my knee would reach.

"You're lying," I declare, trying to force confidence behind my every word. "I'm your mate. You must be attracted to me."

83

"Of course I'm attracted to you. That's not the point. The point is, I'm good at holding myself back from doing something I may regret," he tells me, and I grit my teeth in defiance. I have no idea why this irritates me. At least I can be glad he isn't expecting something from me after coming straight from the forest.

I turn my head slightly, looking off through the trees. "I'm not attracted to you either..."

"I never said I wasn't-"

"Let's keep walking," I snap, slipping out from under his arm. He pauses before following me back down the path while I pretend to admire the vibrant greens of the garden around me. He doesn't speak for a while, and when I glance over to him, he's smiling.

I glare at him defiantly. "What?"

"Hmm?"

"What are you smiling at?" I question further.

"You," he replies.

"Why?"

"You are having a hard time believing that I can't control myself around you," he continues. His smile is infuriating. "You could strip naked right in front of me and I wouldn't make any advancements toward you. I wouldn't even be tempted."

I bit back my 'liar' response again. Right now, I'm not in the mood for his stubbornness, and defiance. Even though his claims irritate me, I know they are probably true

"Let's stop talking about this," I say. "Instead, let's talk about how you're going to let me out for a run sometime in the future."

I need to get my conversation with Fate out of my head.

Not once did I agree with him, so right now, I'm not sealed to anything he has proposed. I don't know what will happen to me if I don't agree to his deal, but I'm putting it off for as long as I possibly can. After hearing everything Rylan has said about being able to resist me, I don't see how I would be able to succeed in Sinful's wish.

"I'm sure we can come to some sort of arrangement that doesn't include you making a run for it," Rylan says.

"My sister is here," I say blandly. "Plus, I have an alpha coming after me to drag me away to my death sentence."

Kaden told me he was going to come back, however, he's late. I'm not complaining though. He haunts my thoughts whenever I close my eyes. Would Fate be true to his word when he said he could help me?

Because I don't know what amount of teasing would ever get the alpha of purity to cave.

Chapter Fifteen

Dawn

The days pass by quickly. Most of which, I spend in my room, trying to hide away from the mortification Rylan put me through when he shut down all chance for Fate's idea to work out. I'm happy only seeing him at mealtimes.

However, staying in my room is starting to have an unwanted effect on me. And by unwanted, I mean I'm tearing my hair out in irritation. Being locked up anywhere is not fun.

For Lucy, though, it is.

Fate did a real number on her. He's managed to convince her that being inside is not only safe, but utterly desirable. Sometimes I'm tempted to slap her across the face to shock some sense into her. It almost seems as though she wears a smile across her face to taunt me.

As long as she is happy though, I remind myself every day.

"Come on," Rylan insists, standing at the foot of my door. I glare at him from where I lie on the bed. Reading books has becoming one of my favorite past times. Stepping into another world completely helps quell my itch to get outside and run around. Luckily for me, Rylan has enough books to supply me with. My expeditions to the library in the early morning are the best part of my day.

"I'm fine here," I reply. Rylan sighs deeply. He is trying to convince me to go out on another walk with him. From past experience, I can tell it doesn't get me anywhere.

He takes a step inside the room, and I feel every part of my body tense up.

"I know you want to," he says with a sly smile. My eyes narrow at him, knowing the game he is trying to play right now. He wants to use my stubborn streak to lure me outside. Why he has such a fascination with leading me back to where I hid from him, I don't know. Part of me wondered if he enjoyed the chase and wants to give me a chance to get away so we can start it all over again.

If so ... I don't want to play.

"Maybe I do," I say warily, swinging my legs to the side of the bed, trying to make sure I wasn't getting too close to Rylan. If he really isn't at all tempted by me, then I'm going to keep my distance. That's either before I decide to take Fate up on his offer, or wait until this whole mate ceremony in a few weeks. "If you would stay here."

"It will be fun," he says warmly, although I doubt every word out of his mouth. "I have something to show you anyway."

"Does it have anything to do with the mate bond that you clearly don't want anything to do with?" I ask, not meaning to sound so spiteful, however, I can't help but get a jab back at him after what he did in the garden a week ago.

Rylan smirks, before moving forward to sit on the edge of my bed.

I watch him warily.

"Are you mad about that?" he asks softly. I can tell he is trying to be serious, but I can hear the humor under his breath. "Does it annoy you that I'm not tempted by you?"

I dismiss him, glancing away defiantly.

"Well, if you have to know, there are many things I want to do to you. I am, though, the alpha of purity, and I know how to hold myself back from my thoughts," he tells me, this time sobering up so I can actually look him in the eye. It still doesn't make me any less irritated at him for his garden antics.

If Fate thinks I'm going to beg Rylan all the way into bed, he has another thought coming.

Then he holds his hand out to me. "Come on then, I promise you might actually like this gift, and if you don't, your sister probably will."

Sighing, I take his hand. This time, his hands are gloriously bare, and the moment my skin touches his, I remember why having a mate is something so many people worship in this pack. The delightful feeling travels up and back down my back, making me unintentionally tighten my grip on him, as if he might slip away.

Of course, he doesn't make any movement to suggest he is at all affected by the sparks elicited by my touch.

He leads me outside again, which is no surprise. It's the only place he can really tempt me out to. There, I can get some distance and maybe even plot an unrealistic escape plan which probably includes Kaden on the other side, waiting to throw me into the back of his car and drive me straight to the discipline pack.

The sun is setting as we walk out. I really lost track of time in my room.

"Want to give me a clue?" I ask, looking across the garden for a hint of something new. Rylan only shakes his head, a slight smile playing on his features.

I had no idea what he had been planning until we walked around the side of the house. It was buried beneath the trees, bathed in the soft glow of sunset oranges and pinks. At the sight of it, I was slightly confused, and then I smiled, letting Rylan's hand go so I could turn and properly face him.

"A swing set?" I say in disbelief, glancing back at it to see if it was truly real. "What use do I have for a swing set?"

Rylan shrugged, walking over to it. It was made of pine wood and metal chains led down from the top to a single seat made for someone of adult size. If Lucy put her small body in there, she

88

would stand no chance. If I did ... Well, I've never had a swing set before, so this is all a foreign concept.

"I can tell you have a hard time relaxing at times. Thought this might be something fun for you to take your mind off of everything you've been through," Rylan comments.

As much as I hate to admit it, my heart swelled a little at that.

Leaving him where he stood, I wandered a little closer to the strange contraption. Touching the edge of the seat, I watched it swing rhythmically back and forth. Normal people would just go and sit on it, but I can't bring myself to do so.

I feel Rylan come up behind me. "Something wrong?"

"I've never really used one before," I tell him honestly. Taking that guard's life was less daunting than a seat that moves when you sit on it. I'm sure Lucy would have jumped right on...

"I figured that much."

Rylan wasn't making fun of me, however, I still wanted to prove to him that I could pull this off. This was a surprisingly nice gesture of him, so I had to at least try. So, holding my breath, I slowly turned around, keeping my gaze on Rylan's while I sat down on the shuddering seat; my hands gripping the chain tightly.

"See, it's not that bad," he says gently, as I sit there, eyes wide and try to figure out whether or not I like it or not. Any wrong move and I might fall backwards. Rylan surely would get a kick out of that.

When he grabs the chains to pull me back enough to swing me, I yelp.

"You're more scared of this than sleeping in a forest at night?" Rylan says in disbelief, unable to keep the smile off his face.

"Forests can't potentially move out from under you when you aren't ready for it," I inform him, still trying to attempt to push myself back enough to actually swing. Rylan still stands close enough to maybe grab me if I fell straight to the dirt. Although, the amused expression on his face suggests he might just watch me fall for the hell of it.

My first real swing is successful. The next, not so much.

My body lurches forward, luckily it's caught by Rylan's expectant arms. Immediately, I'm brought to a stop, my heart beating as if it were a cliff I was falling off, rather than a piece of wood a meter off the ground.

"I suck at being normal," I mutter, looking at my mate who is trying his very best not to laugh at my attempts.

"You're-"

All of a sudden, someone calls Rylan's name from behind us. When he turns around, it's someone with a phone call ready for him. Something about alpha business and how he would be back in a couple of seconds. When he offered to bring me back inside I insisted I would be okay sitting on the swing outside.

Yet again, me trying to prove that I'm more competent than I actually am.

Who knows how long he was waiting for a moment like this to happen, or whether or not he had set it up, but he emerged from the trees right behind me. I didn't know he was there until he spoke in that crisp, foreign accent; one belonging to a vengeance pack member. Alpha Kaden.

"That was quite the show."

Instantly, I'm pushing off the swing unceremoniously. Every ounce of attraction I'd had towards the new contraption diminished as soon as I realized he had been watching me the entire time.

"How long have you been there for?" I question breathlessly.

Kaden smiled at me in a way that had worried shivers dig into my back like claws. The thick wall behind him should have kept the alpha out. Although, I don't doubt his ability to get into Rylan's property.

He then proceeds to shrug as if it's normal to be standing unwelcomed in someone's garden. "Long enough. I only wanted to pass something onto you, Dawn."

I warily watch him step forward.

90

The closer he gets, the more I find myself wanting to run inside to Rylan. I know if I do that, I'm not going to get far. Kaden waited out here to get me alone, and if I ruin that, I'm sure it won't end well. So, I stay rooted to the spot in utter fear of the alpha, trying not to react as he strolls around the swing that looks far too domestic next to him.

"If you're here to take me away, then do it," I say confidently, trying not to be bothered by his sinister eyes. "Leave my sister and Rylan out of it."

"None of that. As I said, I simply want to pass something on to you."

His hand slips into his jacket, pulling out a piece of paper, which is folded up into a small square. He hands it to me, despite my hesitation to touch it.

My entire being wants to toss it over my shoulder. I resist, knowing my defiance will get me nowhere but dead. So, I carefully unfold the paper, smoothing it out enough so I can see the handwritten words upon it.

My heart stops, as I frown, realizing what it spelt out.

A riddle.

Chapter Sixteen

Dawn

The riddle made no sense as I read it in my mind.

Untouchable as unseen,

A ghost of something you'll never be.

See him once, never twice,

And witness something as cold as ice.

Trust someone just as bad,

You don't want to make him mad.

"Is this a warning?" I question. I couldn't see any other explanation for this strange riddle that I had no answer to.

Kaden stayed silent for a while longer before he spoke again, letting me process what was on the note. "I want your answer by midnight. Someone will come for it. If you fail to answer the riddle, they will die. If you answer it correctly, they live."

"Why are you doing this?" I demand angrily, watching him back away from me slowly. "Why not just take me away now? That's the end game, isn't it?"

"I'm testing you," he tells me, before turning his back on me. He pauses before walking away. "Plus, I like a game."

Then he walked away, and I stood there, wondering how I would ever get out of this situation.

***

I'm stuck in my room for a completely different reason tonight.

Honestly, I would much rather be outside on Rylan's swing set, despite how childish it may seem. Kaden's riddle has left me dumbfounded as my mind struggles to find an answer. Rylan told me he enjoys playing games with people and making them stress out at the idea of a riddle that could completely change their future.

And yes, I showed Rylan the riddle. I knew I would never figure it out on my own, however, when I showed Rylan, he knew about as much as I did about it.

"You know what, we shouldn't be thinking about this riddle right now," I muse, sinking my head deeper into the pillow. "We should probably find the person who he's working with, since apparently they are in the estate right now."

Rylan makes a noise of agreement from where he lays casually back across the end of my bed. "I assume it's one of my guards."

The idea of that makes me a little nervous. What if he's right? If Kaden managed to sneak past the wall undetected, then it makes sense for him to have someone working for him within Rylan's home. I just wonder if the guard knows Kaden wants him dead. Maybe if we interrogate them all, we can get one of them to confess to save their own life.

Then who knows what Kaden will do to me…

"This riddle is impossible. Who's supposed to be worse than Kaden, unless the answer actually *is* Kaden," I say, sitting up so I could see Rylan's reaction. He's holding a spare piece of paper that I wrote the riddle on so we both could have a copy.

"No," he dismisses. "That would be too obvious."

I sigh deeply, scraping my hair back over my head. For the first time in a while, I washed my hair. Now it's baby soft and falls in almost every direction possible.

∧

"I just don't understand why he wants to do this to me. I don't even know why he wants me dead."

"Because of me," Rylan says solemnly, pulling himself up to look at me. The look of dismay on his face makes me nervous. Of all things, it would be helpful to know he wasn't worried. "I could take him down in a one-on-one fight, but he would never let a circumstance like that ever happen."

I'm tempted to fight him myself. Of course, that wouldn't end very well on my part.

I kick up off the bed and wander to the window. Evening has fallen over the pack - I have a decent view from where my room is. Seeing the way everything lights up reminds me of home. The desire pack is known for having the city of lights, the city of the night. Maybe one day I'll be able to go back. With Rylan as my mate, I'm not exactly sure that's possible.

"Once Kaden is out of our lives, everything will get better," I hear Rylan say from behind me. I can tell he's stood up. "Then maybe we can work on whatever this relationship is between us."

The last part is frightening.

I'm probably one of the most inexperienced people in that field. I may have had some kind of kid boyfriend back in the desire pack, but ever since we left, I never thought twice about it. Well, that was until I met Rylan, and all my nerves in that sector of my life caught up to me. Maybe that's one of the reasons why I ran away with Lucy.

"Right." I breathe. He's come up beside me, looking out the window with me. "Our relationship, which won't exist when Kaden kills me."

Rylan chuckles, despite the heaviness of the situation. He's probably amused with the snarky attitude I can't help but adopt whenever I'm under pressure. At least Fate isn't weighing on my mind constantly which he was before.

"Should we go torture some guards together?"

My eyes widen as I glance at him, only admiring the rising flush against his face for a single moment. "Torture?"

His eyes gleam when he turns to me. This must be the exact look he gave the Elites when he told them to go out and do

94

whatever they could to get me back; like beating innocent girls and killing innocent people.

"Okay, maybe a little negotiation," he reforms, his lips slanting into a coy smile I wasn't about to fall for.

"That sounds better-"

"Says the one who killed one of my guards…"

"Okay," I growl. "That was purely an accident. He threw himself at me, and I had no other choice."

Rylan tilts his head, the smile on his face irritating me. "Sure."

Gritting my teeth, another growl of irritation rises in my throat. He wants to be infuriating? Fine, he can be infuriating on his own. Just as I go to turn my back in him, he grabs my arm, swinging me back against him so I have to look straight at him. I try to be a little defiant and look away, but he's quick to cup my chin and force me to look at him. At least now he's being slightly more serious.

He takes me by surprise as he leans forward, gently kissing my forehead. It's a new kind of electricity between us. A kind that has my skin shivering with excitement.

"What was that for?" I question, sounding awfully breathless.

He shrugs loosely. "For being my mate."

***

I stand at the doorway, my eyes brushing over the line of guards that Rylan has lined up right in front of me.

"Now," he says calmly. "We have a few things to discuss."

Rylan's demeanour is completely different around his guards, I've decided. He's all the more alpha, as he sets his shoulders back and walks with a sharp stare that makes me a little nervous, and I'm not even the one he's dealing with. I wouldn't want to be a guard standing in that line right now.

"It seems as though one of you is working with the alpha of vengeance; Alpha Kaden."

My eyes skim over their faces. Plenty of them have half their faces covered by dark cloth; apparel that I've come to realize is a part of their uniform. The problem with that, is that I can't see their expressions to tell if they are guilty. All of them cast their gazes to the floor as respect.

"Whoever you are, I suggest you comes forward, as your life is in danger," Rylan says coolly. His attitude it intriguing as he addresses them without a slip in his indifference.

Not a single guard makes a move.

"And it's not me you should worry about. In fact, I'll be happy to send you home with no consequences," Rylan continues, trying to tempt them out at this point. "You see, Kaden wants you dead, and he's going to kill you at midnight if you fail the job you have been assigned by him."

Again, no one moves.

A horrific thought seeps into my mind. What if the guard already knows their fate? What if this is a suicide mission they are completely aware of?

Rylan goes to speak, however, he's cut off as a female guard stumbles forward.

She's shoves the cloth down her face, revealing who she is. Clearly, her soft features show a purity pack member. Tears stream down her face as she falls to her knees in front of Rylan.

"Please, I have a family," she breathes, hiccupping through her tears. "I don't want to die."

Immediately Rylan is helping her up, and I'm at her side. At the same time as being in sympathy for her and her family, I'm curious how Kaden convinced her into this. The more we can know about his tactics, the better off I will be in defending myself against him.

"You're safe now," Rylan reassures her. "I promise."

***

I glance at the note by my bed stand that night. It's haunting me, even though I know Kaden's little guard has been caught, and is

96

being kept in a safe, monitored room where she can't touch me, and Kaden can't touch her.

Rylan had only just retired for the night, after spending over an hour with me in my room, trying to get to the bottom of the riddle. He's seriously troubled by it.

Irritated, I snatch the note and stand.

I'm done with it. I'm done with the stress it has given me, and I want all this over. So, I crumple the note up, slide the window open and toss it out. One of the gardeners will find it in a bush below tomorrow. Maybe one of them will be able to figure out the riddle.

I close the window, just as I hear the door open, and then close again.

It's a guard.

They lean back against the door, looking up at me with dark eyes. Chills streak down my back as I stumble back until I'm against the window. guards aren't allowed in our room. This guard is clearly here for another reason.

Then he tugs the cloth down his face. The familiarity fills me with anger. Kace; it's Kaden's brother.

His smile is triumphant.

"I've come to collect the answer to the riddle!"

Chapter Seventeen

Dawn

I didn't know how to react. All I could do was think about how my life was probably about to end in the next few seconds and in my own room.

"What are you doing here?" I questioned faintly. I didn't know what to say that might help me in this situation. I'm trapped in my room by a member of the vengeance pack, who also happens to be the brother of the alpha himself. I'm done for.

Especially since I never thought I would actually need the answer to the riddle.

"I said that I'm here to collect the answer to the riddle," Kace repeats, taking a casual step closer to me. Every muscle in my body tensed.

"You?" I confirm shakily. "We caught the guard who works for Kaden. She confessed."

It made sense in my mind, but I had to confirm it. After all my hiding in the forest, I'd learned the enemy's technique. Now, I could see Kaden's right in front of my face. His backup plan was Kace, who clearly was working undercover here without any of us knowing. The girl was just another part of his messed up plan. Her job was to confess, to be caught.

All to get an answer out of me.

"Of course that poor guard. She'll be the one to die if you fail to answer the riddle correctly," Kace muses, wandering over to my dresser. I wish I had a weapon. Any weapon. That way I could crush that air of arrogance he's carrying around with him.

He suddenly turned back to me, his expression was dressed in a smirk. "And by the look of horror on your face, I can safely assume you don't have one."

I sober my expression. No use spelling what I'm thinking out to Kace. At the moment, I'm doing everything to at least remember the riddle to formulate an answer. I have to at least guess, otherwise I'm killing another innocent person. From what I can gather, the riddle is about someone in high power. I decide I may just have an answer.

"You shouldn't jump to conclusions," I reply.

Kace chuckles. He's too busy looking around the room to be bothered with me it seems. For whatever reason, he's captivated by the simplicity of it all. Perhaps the room design is different in the vengeance pack. Either that, or Kace has been living as poorly as I have.

"So, the answer then?" He prompts, raising an eyebrow as if to call me out, to make a fool of me. He knows I have nothing substantial.

"Alpha Kaden. I believe the answer to the riddle is Alpha Kaden."

Kace looks thoughtful for a moment. He stalks over to me. There's a window behind me, which he brushes past to open. Stumbling back a few steps, I use his confusing movements to my advantage. I don't need an explanation for his gesture towards the window.

I need a weapon.

"Why do you think that's the answer?" He asks, leaning his hand against the sill as he gazes out.

Casting a single glance in direction, I note his lack of attention on me. Less importantly, I happen to notice the way his dark hair flutters softly in the gentle breeze. Shaking my head, I back up until I hit my dresser. With trembling hands, I unscrew one of the handles and clutch it in my fist behind my back.

"It speaks of a fearful leader. I assume it's in the point of view of one of his pack members, perhaps," I murmur, glancing toward the door. I could make a run for it instead of facing him. "Or maybe from your point of view."

I knew it contradicted part of the riddle, however, I had no other answer. Anyway, I was too busy weighing up my options. Kace remained staring out the window. I could use the nail sticking out from the handle to stab him, to stun him before running. If I get out the door now, I might have a chance. The problem is, I'll be leading him to Lucy's room, which is right next to mine.

"Fair answer," I hear Kace barely whisper. His words catch on the breeze.

There's a moment's silence. Perhaps I could have used it to my advantage better, however, I still didn't know what to do. Kace is either in the same position, or is trying to make this situation worse for me. The latter suits him a little better.

"It can't be fun living in your brother's shadow," I say calmly, taking a step closer to him. I've decided I'm going to stun him and run. For now, I have to keep his concentration on my words.

"I have no problem with it."

"But listening to everything he says? Why does he get to make all the decisions?"

At this point, I'm right behind him. Maybe I was stupid to think he would believe I wanted to help him in some way, or at least point out the problems in his life that need solving. The moment I raised my fist to stab the nail into his back, he turned suddenly, grabbing my wrist and my waist.

His eyes are burning. "You think I'm a good person?"

The handle drops out of my hand from the pressure on my wrist as Kace turns me around, almost pushing me completely out the window. The cold air sucks the breath out of me. This pack may not be as cold as the desire pack, but it still has an icy bite to it in the dead of night.

"I could push you out this window without a second thought," he reminds me. My eyes are trained to the ground below, which is lit by the garden lights. I wouldn't survive if I fell head first out. Maybe feet first I would only break my ankles. It would be a different fate if it were my neck breaking.

Maybe he would have done it, had he not heard my bedroom door opening. As he turned to look at who had intruded, he pulled me back in, nearly causing me to hit my head on the window pane. It was Rylan. How he knew I was in trouble, I have no idea. His presence was enough to frighten Kace as he violently pushed me toward Rylan, before he swung straight out the window.

"He's going to escape," I said quickly, pushing off Rylan, whose chest I had ran into. When I looked back out of the window, Kace was gone. Had he even hit the ground? Surviving that fall would be impossible for anyone else, but I knew he had escaped death.

"Don't worry, let's not think about that right now," Rylan says, him calmness mildly infuriating.

"What about the other guard? Is she okay?" I question, remembering the threats Kace made to her. She was just a pawn in Kaden's game. Just like Kace is.

Rylan looks grim. "Her death is what alerted me. I came here as soon as I found out."

My jaw clenched as I sat back up on my bed. How could I let this happen? If I had spent more time trying to figure out what the answer to the riddle was, then the guard would have survived, and I wouldn't nearly have had my life taken by Kace. I probably wasn't even close to the answer and now I would never find out.

"Are there guards searching for who killed her?" I ask, annoyed that he had put me above everyone else in this place.

"She killed herself, Dawn," he tells me softly, sitting beside me on the bed.

I close my eyes. Of course. She had strict instructions from Kaden. Suicide was her plan the entire time, so her fright when she first came forward was most probably genuine. Knowing Kaden, he was threatening her family, or someone close to her. A punishment worse than her own death.

"This isn't going to happen again, okay?" Rylan promises, his arm coming around me as comfort. I comply, feeling too tired and depressed to fight anything anymore. "I'll make sure of it."

"It's Kaden," I grumble against his chest.

"Yes, but you don't know Kaden like I do," he tells me. "I have something coming for him. Trust me."

***

The next morning, everything was awfully grim. Lucy didn't feel like joining us for breakfast. Instead, she wanted to sleep in.

So it was just Rylan and I.

"You don't look so good this morning," he says from the other side of the table, watching me with concern. "Are you feeling okay?"

I'm not sure if it's after what happened last night that has made me feel ill, but it's definitely something. So far, I've been blaming being nearly thrown out the bedroom window for my spinning head and queasy stomach. Either that, or the rich food I'm not used to eating, and the late night last night have caught up to me and my body is protesting.

I push my plate away. "I think I need to stop eating so much."

Rylan chuckles. As my eyes drifted back to my plate, I felt like I'd just been punched in the stomach. I pushed my chair out, knowing I was about to throw up any second if I didn't make it to the bathroom in time.

"Woah, Dawn, what's wrong?" Rylan questions. I ignore him, pulling away from the table to make a run for it, pretending I didn't nearly spill all my breakfast all over the table.

I hardly make it to the bathroom. As my stomach turned over completely, I wondered why I was so sick. I haven't thrown up for years. It must be this domestic lifestyle I'm not used to.

Rylan came in to hold my hair back at some point. By the time I was finished, my entire body was trembling and I felt disgraceful.

Rylan was giving me a nervous look; one that told me he was more frightened than I was.

Something is truly wrong with me. Something neither of us have the answer to.

Chapter Eighteen

Dawn

"We have no other explanation. All my doctors are dumbfounded. I'm willing to do anything to find out what is wrong, otherwise I'm going to lose her."

Rylan didn't think I could hear him from where I lay in bed, but I could; he left the door open slightly, so I could even see the concern on his face. I didn't know who he was calling, but I knew it was his way of trying to save my life. He won't tell me directly that my life is on the line, but I know it.

I feel it.

My entire body aches dully; a constant reminder of the fact that I'm being kept in bed with very few exceptions to get up. My stomach is in a constant state of nausea, which has stripped down the amount of hours I've slept, as well as the amount of food and water I've had during these last few days.

I'm dying, I don't doubt it. Rylan surely thinks so, even if he won't tell me. All the doctors who visit and say this isn't anything to do with a basic stomach problem believe I'm going to die too. At this point, I just lie here, accepting it.

"I can't take her out of this pack unless I know there will be a certain cure," Rylan says desperately. I see him pacing. "I would appreciate if you could come for one visit, just to see what is wrong."

Now I'm curious.

Who is visiting me? I assume another useless doctor who will give me a dumbfounded look and tell Rylan he can't explain it. Maybe if Rylan makes it public, someone will be able to figure out what is wrong, or maybe even someone else who is suffering will have answers. Right now, I can't think of a single person who would have any idea.

"Thank you Malik, I appreciate it," I hear Rylan say, before he hangs the phone up.

Malik, as in Alpha Malik, the alpha of love? I know very little about him, including his medical knowledge, but I must admit he doesn't seem like the kind of man to know how to diagnose me, or even cure me.

When Rylan walked back into the room, he looked bothered. His hair was more unruly than I'm used to. I found out over this past week that he had a habit of running his hand through his hair when stressed. He did it to the point where his hair becomes scattered across his forehead and ears.

"Malik, huh?"

Rylan sighs deeply, coming to sit beside me on the bed. I've told him to stay away plenty of times, being worried that he would catch whatever I have. Of course, he has refused, however, he doesn't let Lucy get too close.

"He has books that explain many medical issues we don't have the answer to. Most of them are in a language originally spoken in the love pack, which Malik was taught before he became an alpha. He is one of the only people who can read them, and can find out what might be wrong with you," Rylan explains.

I shake my head. "I don't understand how something so unique could happen to me."

"I know. We will figure out why," Rylan says, and I close my eyes in irritation.

My mind has a hard time concentrating on things, since it is too busy noticing how much pain I'm in. It's not a familiar pain either. I've never felt this way before, and I hate it. The confusion is almost as bad as the constant need to hold myself back from throwing up.

"If he lives up to all the rumors I have heard about him, I'll be angry."

Rylan chuckles. "Don't worry, he has a mate now. And so do you, remember?"

Malik arrives the next day. Luckily enough, the purity pack is close to the love pack, so it didn't take as long for him to get here as it would from anywhere else in the pack quarter. It was Rylan who thanked him profusely when he came in, a single book tucked under his arm. At this point, I'm a little too delirious to truly take notice of everything happening around me.

I've seen him plenty of times on television around two years ago, when I still lived in the desire pack. He held some kind of competition to find aluna. I wonder if it ever did work out for him, since he ended up finding his true mate.

"Dawn, how are you feeling?" he asks as he walks in. I have enough energy to give him a deadpan look.

He is quite a handsome guy, with these piercing blue eyes that are so incredibly electric that it's hard to believe they're natural. He looks like a typical love pack member, if I'm perfectly honest. Those soft features and beautiful eyes can only be found in one place.

"As bad as I probably look," I reply, hoping he wasn't about to judge the hoarseness of my voice. I sound like I've spent the last week singing songs constantly.

"You don't look half as bad as you think, for someone who is apparently sick."

Malik's compliment, if it could be considered that, brushed straight over my head. He's most likely saying that to make me feel better about facing my impending death. By the uncomfortable look on the man's face, he already knew what was wrong with me, and didn't want to tell me around Rylan, who had only just walked in through the door.

106

If I'm honest, Rylan looks sicker than I do. All the worry about me has done that to him, while I've lain in bed, vomiting every now and again.

"So, apparently you have a magical book that tells you stuff."

"Exclude the magical part," he says with a slight smile, sitting on the edge of my bed. Rylan keeps to the wall, giving Malik space to do whatever he needs to do. The thick book balances on his lap, looking awfully intimidating. It might have the means to answer what is wrong with me. To solve what has everyone so afraid of me …

"Do you know?" I ask tentatively. "What's wrong with me?"

Malik looks grim as he shrugs. Both Rylan and I watch curiously as Malik opens the book. The dialect is strange, however, the alpha of love seems to have no trouble deciphering the meaning as his finger brushes under the words. He skipped to a certain part of the book which made me guess that he had some idea of what could be the problem.

There is several minutes silence, as he looks at me and then to the book, trying to figure out where I fit on the pages. Eventually, he sighs, closing the book.

"I have two possible answers," he says.

Rylan and I stay silent, waiting for him to explain himself.

"It could be poisoning. Dawn would have thrown up to the point where the poison has gotten out of her system. Of course, she will need specific technology to rehabilitate quickly and safely," Malik explains.

I glance at Rylan, knowing exactly what he meant by technology. He seemed to know also. "She needs to be taken to the wisdom pack."

"Yes. That is the only pack I can think of that can cure her of this poisoning before it gets worse, if it does. You can never be so sure," Malik tells us. I've never been to the wisdom pack before, and actually, know very little about it. I know everyone is

107

extremely intelligent, and the entire pack is quite secretive about their technological advancements.

"What's the other option?" I question.

"I've only dealt with this once before, with the luna of the devotion pack, of all people," Malik tells me. I frown, knowing very little about her. "She caught a disease passed on by a desire pack member."

A desire pack member? Lucy is the only desire pack member I have been around for over a year now. The likelihood of either of us having a dormant issue like that is low, although, I'm not the one who knows so much.

Seeing my confusion, Malik continues. "Have you been touched by anyone of unknown origin lately? Thea presented different symptoms to you, however, there are numerous ones that perhaps haven't had the chance to occur yet. She had an experience with a man who touched her, who really shouldn't have."

Malik glanced over to Rylan as he talked, who was looking at me with narrowed eyes. Swallowing, I look down at my fingers. Rylan expected me to say no, I knew it.

"Yes, actually, I did."

"Anyone can be given the disease to be passed on," Malik says. I frown, remembering the way Rylan touched me over the past few days. "alphas are immune, as far as I'm aware."

"Can we find out who touched her?" Rylan growled, cutting in.

I shake my head at him. "It was nothing. Some guy from your pack of purity nearly raped me, however, I managed to get away."

There was no way I was about to mention Kace. That would mean explaining the fact that I had accepted a coat from him that ended up leading Kaden straight to me. Rylan wouldn't care that I stuffed up, however, it weighed on my shoulders all the time. Lucy and I could be in the freedom pack by now.

"Seriously-"

A furious Rylan was cut off by Malik.

"You need to make your decision on how you are going to continue from now on," he said, looking at both me and Rylan.

"How can we cure the disease?" I ask.

Malik visibly cringes. "There are repercussions I'm not sure you will want to hear. Thea was able to live, due to having a very Phantom mate."

Phantoms. Another thing I knew very little about. They were creatures of myth, which no one ever bothered to inform me on. I'm lucky with that though, apparently, since I heard they give people nightmares. Perks of having no friends, I suppose.

"So,   you're   saying   I'm   going   to   die?"

"Only unless you truly have the second option. There is always the first," Malik offers.

Rylan pushes away from the wall before Malik even has the opportunity to finish his sentence. "We are taking her to the wisdom pack right now. We are going to visit Alpha Alden."

Chapter Nineteen

Dawn

My entire body was draped across the backseat as Rylan drove and Malik sat in the passenger seat.

The moment I was out of the house, my head cleared and I began to feel a little better. Seconds after that, I threw up, confirming this that this wasn't a normal disease, and that Malik was right, as absurd as that may seem. So, we have decided our best bet is to head to the wisdom pack, where Alpha Alden would be able to aid us.

"Are you feeling okay?" Rylan asks, for the fifteenth time this drive.

I've slept most of the way. The wisdom pack is above the equator, in the warmer part of the pack quarter. It is still a mild pack though, being quite close to the purity pack. That means the drive won't be so long.

"My stomach still hurts," I tell him blandly. "But I don't feel like I'm going to faint at every moment."

"We are nearly at the base of the wisdom pack," Rylan assures me.

Looking out the window from my angle is difficult. I can only see the sky, so there is no way I can tell where we are. Being too afraid that moving will disrupt whatever is happening in my body, I stay lying down, feeling the vibrations of the car as we drive. I'm not sure how long we have been driving, or how long I've slept for, so everything feels somewhat dazed and confusing.

We drive for what feels like hours, although by the length of Malik and Rylan's discussions, it can't have been that long. I'm not blaming the feeling of the wait on the sickness, but on how boring their talking actually was. Alpha and pack business really isn't all that interesting.

As I was dozing in and out of sleep, Rylan's voice woke me.

"We're here."

This time, I force my body up, curious to see what the wisdom pack looks like. I've heard little about this, so of course, I'm curious.

I'm amazed. This is nothing like the desire pack, or even the purity pack. Massive skyscrapers surrounded us for as far as the eye can see, looking awfully futuristic and like something out of a film. Being submerged in what looks a pack that is an entire business district should be frightening for someone like myself, however, I'm too awed to feel anything else right now.

"The wisdom pack is at a clear advantage over every pack, however, we are lucky the alpha behind this place is a kind man," Rylan tells me, noticing how my fingers press against the glass as I can't get enough of the sight. A part of me wants to explore, if I was in better condition, while another part wants to hide from it.

"The average person here could out beat us all in a battle of knowledge, although, many of them are very humble about it," Malik adds.

Everyone walking the streets is dressed smartly. Nobody here would ever commit a crime.

They are too intelligent for that.

Even the streets are clean, with every store front immaculate, and every building looking sparkling, clean and brand new. A part of me thinks it might just be a trick of the eyes that some wisdom pack member is projecting to mess with me. The technology here is always advancing, with the scraps of it all going to our packs. Nothing that they could do would surprise me.

111

"Where does Alpha Alden reside?" I ask, trying to speak smoothly, rather than cough up my words.

Malik and Rylan exchange glances.

"Somewhere on the top floor of one of these buildings," Rylan says, pointing at the massive skyscrapers that definitely keep to their namesake. "He moves around a lot. He gave us an address that is always different when anyone is visiting."

Immediately, I'm taken aback. I wonder why he does that. I'm probably the last person he would tell, I'm sure.

The main street is cramped with cars looking like advanced models of every car I have ever seen. I can't take my eyes off them, and the people in them before Rylan pulls to the side of the road. At the same time, as I'm desperate to get out of this car and see what the stores around here offer, or what the apartments look like, I'm worried I might throw up on something nice and expensive.

"This might be it," Rylan says, sounding wary.

I can tell why. No guards or security can be seen anywhere in front of the building. People move in and out of it as if an alpha doesn't reside somewhere on the top floor.

Rylan and Malik step out before me. As Rylan tries to help me out of the car, I brush him off, trying to test my own feet out on the smooth pavement beneath me. Nausea doesn't follow me from the car, however, a splitting headache decides to take its place.

Breathing in the fresh air, as balmy as it seems, is a relief, nonetheless.

Walking into the lobby, I do decide to stand close to Rylan, ready to catch onto his waiting arm if it comes down to it. Right now, my only painful infliction is the headache.

The entire atmosphere of the place is different to anything I have ever seen. The modern grey and white palette used by whoever designed this, is very effective. No one else in the small area near the reception desk seems to notice; they're probably all very used to it.

I, on the other hand, look slightly insane as I try take note of the secrets of the wisdom pack. Not many people can just get in here without special invitation.

Lucky Rylan is an alpha, and knows one.

"We go straight upstairs," Rylan murmurs in my ear, catching my attention. "Don't make eye contact with any of them."

I knew he meant the people walking in and out, but I'm not sure why. I can guess though. My educated guess is that they are wealthy, and I'm not, and I shouldn't so much as waste their time by doing anything to draw attention to me. Instead I keep my eyes on their outfits.

I'm not sure why all these incredibly intelligent people are so beautiful. With flawless complexions and perfect bodies, I have to wonder what technology makes them look this way. The woman who just brushed past me would have been considered a doll in the purity pack, and even the desire pack.

We take an elevator up; the first foreign thing I've stepped into so far. The feeling of it moving under me has my head spinning, so I don't hesitate to lean on Rylan like a crutch.

"This will fix things, I promise," Rylan says, wrapping his arm around my shoulders. I couldn't be grateful, even though when I glance at Malik, he looks somehow doubtful. Does he know something we don't? Maybe he thinks this trip is useless, or that the other option he presented earlier is truly the answer, but he doesn't want to break to either of us.

The elevator door opens quickly, making us jump.

"That went on forever," I breathe, not letting go of Rylan's arm as we make our way down the corridor.

The carpet is a strange pastel blue color, and the walls are off-white. No one is around this time, which I'm grateful for. I don't have to feel intimidated, and I can look wherever I want, whenever I want. I'm sure that behind each door we pass, there are plenty of rich people waiting to judge me if they ever saw me.

113

"Where is he?" I decide to ask, training my gaze on Malik's back, as he walks in front of us. He holds a small piece of paper, ready to knock upon whatever door conceals the alpha of wisdom.

"Could be anywhere," Rylan muses, "he's Alden, after all."

I have no idea what that means, considering I've never met the guy.

Malik finds his door right at the end of the hallway. For a single, white stained door, it's awfully intimidating. Malik doesn't look fazed at all as he knocks twice on the door, and leans against the frame casually. Rylan and I stand back, myself leaning on him, ready to use him as a shield in case this Alpha is as aggressive as the others.

The door opens. It's a girl, dressed immaculately in a suit, her hair loose around her shoulders. Her style is mixture of casual and business, which I can't quite wrap my head around.

"Your guests have arrived," she says over her shoulder, before she stands back to let us in.

Nervously, I follow with Rylan into the room, smiling at the girl as a greeting. She looks away with dismissal. She has that wisdom pack look; sleek, dark brown hair and blue eyes.

I focus my attention on the apartment secondly. It's open plan, with the opposite wall being an entire window of glass; showing the cityscape for miles. The floor is wooden and lustrous, going from where we stand to the kitchen. Like everything else here, it's new, bright and expensively modern. Oh, and I can already spot several pieces of technology I've never seen before.

But what I really notice, is the man leaning back on a chaise lounge in front of us, looking out the window.

"Alden," Malik says brightly, walking confidently toward the man. "You skipped the last alpha meeting."

Yes, the alpha meeting. The exclusive meeting held monthly for all alphas to discuss matters and keep the peace. Something I hope to learn about. If Alpha Alden can figure out what is wrong with me, that is.

"You know, things come up," he says, standing swiftly.

His accent is like satin gliding down my arm as the smooth silk of the alpha's voice intoxicated me.

Alden is the epitome of a wisdom pack member, of course. As he strides toward us, I see the smooth, ageless skin, with no lines or blemishes. I see the radiant, sleek dark hair and strange colored eyes. They are almost navy, darkened to the point where they could be black, if it weren't for the subtle hint of blue there. It all ties in with his contemporary dark suit that seems like some recent trend I'll never learn about.

He doesn't stop, as his eyes meet mine. He brushes past an awaiting Malik, and walks toward me with valour, knowing *exactly* what he wants.

I was taken aback by the confidence and the scent of him, as he clasped my chin, and lifted it up so that I was looking straight into his shining eyes.

"You're going to die," he tells me clearly.

Chapter Twenty

Dawn

I pull away from Alden's grasp in fright.

His words had my mind spinning, and for a moment, I thought I would die right there. It was Alden who caught me, his arms coming up to steady me. Wild, vibrant colors crawl across his face, which is etched with concern. In that moment, I was certain I would faint in his arms, however, Rylan was at my side in a second; his hands steadying my arms and back.

Like an instant relief, my muscles relaxed and my mind righted itself. The fog was clearing and drawing the colors and vision manipulation away. I was left feeling sick to my stomach.

"She needs rest," Alden murmurs, taking a step back as I lean closer to Rylan, trying to make sense of what he had said. *I'm going to die?*

"We need an explanation," Rylan says, speaking my words for me.

Alden didn't say anything, as he walked past Malik again, standing directly in front of the couch. That moment of sympathy and concern was gone in a second. An alpha's attitude had taken its place. A cold, indifferent alpha who looked like he had a job to do, and nothing else. He gave me no indication of what he was thinking. He looked like he could get away with murder.

"She needs to sit down on this couch," Alden said coolly, nodding in front of him. "Bring her down to sit here so I can look at her."

Rylan didn't hesitate. If there was someone he was going to trust here, it's Alden. His intelligence is incomparable to anything we have. He's wise, and if he says I'm going to die, that means I'm going to die. But I'm not going to leave this place until I figure when, and why, and how I can stop that from happening.

With shuddering steps, I walk towards the couch with Rylan's assistance.

Alden watches me with an impassive expression, seeming completely detached from emotion as I sink into his insanely comfortable couch. As soon as I'm seated, Alden brushes Rylan off, much to his disgust, before kneeling down in front of me.

Alden stares into my eyes for a few moments, before his gaze drifts down my face, down my body. The silence is thick with anticipation as I remain frigid under his scrutiny. He brings his baby smooth hands up, running them across my jaw, down my neck and to my arms with gentle precision. I'm not sure what this examination is supposed to reveal, but I make no move to protest.

Trembling slightly under his fingertips, I keep my eyes on his face. It's strange seeing him frown with concentration, yet it doesn't disrupt the flawless perfection of his skin. Only a very slight line between his brows can give evidence to the fact that he investigating something without an answer.

Then he makes a noise of confirmation in his throat and takes his hands off my skin.

"My initial assumption is correct. You will die, and there are very little options to prevent that," Alden says solemnly, gracefully standing again.

I'm not sure how I should feel at that announcement. Part of me had expected the moment I had thrown up in the toilet. I know my body is rejecting something, I just didn't know what. Looking at Alden, I can see, no matter how hard he tries to cover it up, that he knows what is wrong with me, and how it happened. His eyes betray him of that much.

"No, that's not possible," Rylan says quickly. Malik doesn't say a word; he already knew. "How could that even happen?"

Alden's tone is accusatory, "I think that's for your mate to explain."

"I would like to know what is wrong with me first," I say defensively. I can feel a mixture of emotion from the males standing around me. Malik doesn't want any part of it, Alden seems to think I've done something bad, and Rylan is worried out of his mind. As I sit here, the news of my fate doesn't sink in, but it weights heavy on my shoulders.

Alden sighs. "You have contracted a disease, as I'm sure you're aware. Perhaps you can inform us of how you got that, or maybe Rylan can, if he is aware. This is incurable."

My jaw clenches at the recycled information.

"Be honest with me," I say hoarsely, "tell me everything."

Alden looks at Rylan, as if for confirmation, and sighs. This alpha is my last chance at survival. If it's over, I want to know, so that I can spend the last s of my life in the forest; in freedom where I belong.

"The root of the disease can come from a single touch. It's very rare, and the symptoms can be presented in various ways; from rashes, to stomach pains, to seizures and debilitating migraines. In your case, you have nausea and dizzy spells, from what I have heard. There is no cure for the disease at this point, however, we are working on one that will be readily available in the next few years."

"How do I have long left?"

"A week or so."

That hit me straight in the chest. I grab the couch cushions, squeezing them in my fists. In the next week? That means there is no chance for me to get this medicine in time. When I glance up at Rylan, his face is ashen.

"How sure are you that this is actually this disease you speak of? It happened so fast," Rylan said slowly.

"Sallow, discolored skin, trembling fingers and lazy eyes, erratic breath and cold-"

Rylan puts his hand up, making Alden pause.

"I can tell you that you could have contracted the disease years ago. In some cases, it can happen moments after you have received the bug, and in others, they take years to actually get sick," Alden tells me.

"You said there were options. What are they?" I decide to ask. I'm not sure how I've managed to sound so rational hearing all this come from Alden's mouth. He doesn't bother sugar-coating it, and I'm glad. His clinical attitude may cause this feeling of impending doom to sink in deeper, but no one else would tell me the truth.

"We have technology that can freeze your body and wake you when a treatment is available," Alden offers.

Instantly, I shake my head. Be kept in a freezer for a few years? That sounds terrible. Who knows how much of life I would miss, or even what I would wake up to. I can't imagine anything worse than that.

Noticing my expression, Alden continues, "You can donate your body to science-"

"No," Rylan and I say at the same time.

"Your last option is to kill yourself," Alden says carefully, causing my eyes to widen. "And we have a phantom wolf turn you."

My heart almost stopped at this. The only phantom wolf I had heard of is Alpha Jasper of the devotion pack. Turning into something of myths isn't only terrifying, but not an option. What would that mean for Lucy? Rylan? What if I couldn't control myself from turning into a wolf that kills people every night?

I know little of the process of turning someone into a phantom wolf. I know I would have to die, to be brought back by a single bite. The whole idea seems ... daunting.

119

"And that's it?" I say in disbelief.

Alden nods. "Would you like some hard liquor?"

"That won't be necessary," Rylan cuts in, coming round to help me off the couch. "Thank you for your hospitality. Do you mind if we stay? It is getting late."

"Of course. There are a couple of rooms down the hallway to your left. Who's sharing?"

I turn to glance at Malik and he holds his hands up.

"Dawn and I will. Again, thank you," Rylan says, helping toward the hallway.

Before I could go, Malik grabbed my arm, pulling me to a stop. He seemed nervous about this. I know he knew that that Thea girl went through what I was, so I could tell he had bad memories tied to it. I can't imagine what, but I'm not about to ask either.

"The girl, Thea, will be willing to help you. She can get here by tomorrow, if you would like to talk to her," Malik offers.

I nod gratefully. "Thank you, Malik."

Maybe she will be able to make the idea actually seem appealing. I can't imagine turning into a natural born killer would be at all attractive. What if it puts Lucy in danger, or I even lash out at Rylan at some point? He and I are supposed to be *trying* with our mate bond, and I have suddenly contracted some kind of disease.

The room for Rylan and me is lavish. There is something about the modern look, with the off-white color palette and wooden furniture that I quite like. It's different to the classic look from the purity pack that I've gotten used to.

"Do you need anything?" Rylan asks, as I take a trembling seat on the edge of the bed.

I feel too sick to eat or drink anything right now. "I'm fine, don't worry."

Rylan comes to sit next to me. Honestly, his presence has my shoulders relaxing and my breath evening out. I want him to touch me, in any way, but I keep my mouth shut. I doubt he would do it,

120

even if I ask. And right now, I'm not really in the best of shape to try tempt him into something. He's probably repulsed by my sickness.

"That's the thing, Dawn," he says softly, pulling a piece of my hair back from my face. I look up into his silvery blue eyes as he speaks. "I do get worried."

I place my hand on his leg. He watches the movement carefully. "If something does happen to me, Rylan, please look after my sister."

He shakes his head at me, grabbing my face between his hands.

"Don't say that. Everything will be fine. Thea will come tomorrow, and we will see how being a Phantom isn't a bad thing. She can help you," Rylan says. I must admit, his optimism isn't catching on.

"In the worst case scenario, can you promise to look after her and yourself? I don't deserve you, I know, and I hope that you will be able to get over my death, if it is to come … " I reason.

Rylan opens his mouth to protest, but I shake my head at him.

"Promise me."

He exhales slowly. "I promise."

Chapter Twenty-One

Dawn

I got next to no sleep that night.

The bed was almost too luxurious, the room too foreign and the bed clothes I'd been provided with were too slippery. Every time Rylan made a single movement in his sleep, I would slide closer to him unintentionally. He would grumble and try to wrap his arms around me before I would try sidle away.

It was an entire routine throughout the night. Not only was I spending the night trying to stay away from his gloriously warm body, but my head ached and my stomach churned constantly.

At one point, I slept, then woke again.

Evidently, gravity and Rylan's wandering hands played a part in our proximity. My back pressed securely against his chest and his arm draped lazily over my waist. His warmth seeped blissfully through my bed clothes, allowing me a few moments to consider staying in bed with him for another hour. His scent was pleasant and addictive, making it all the more difficult to peel the covers back and step out of bed.

Rylan barely shifts at my movement and I'm grateful for that much, at least. I want a few moments to myself before I have to deal with the realities of my sickness.

My stomach twists uncomfortably once my feet are planted on the ground. It has gotten to the point where it's more annoying than anything. The sickness itself hasn't gotten any better, however, I'm becoming more accustomed to living with it. I just can't wait until everything is cured, and I can go back to living how I used to.

With a mate now, though.

I find a bathroom beyond one of the two doors in the room. It's clean, unused and colored a blue like Alden's eyes. I wonder what he typically does during the day. Being an alpha for such a progressive pack can't be easy.

I move back into the bedroom with silent steps, raiding the dresser that Alden has offered to fill for me with clothes typical of this pack's fashion. I find a pair of velvet shorts and a matching long sleeve shirt, made out of a delicate velvet that's an untainted white. I tuck them under my arm and wander back into the bathroom, switching the shower on as I breeze past.

When I look in the mirror, I'm appalled at my own sickly skin and dark circles. My eyes look lifeless and drained. I look away before I can make myself sick, instead concentrating on the wonder of this bathroom.

Why does *everything* have to be so technologically advanced?

Shedding my bedclothes, I slide the glass of the shower door open, watching it fold back magically. There are three showerheads, which is a bizarre concept, as they seem to be controlled with one temperature gauge. As I step under the satiny soft curtain of water, I feel my muscles relax.

By the time I'm finished, I've washed my hair and my entire body with this jasmine scented soap and shampoo, which I delight in. My headache may refuse to cease, but at least I don't smell like Rylan anymore. I won't be so distracted.

Dressing in the clothes left for me, I realize they fit perfectly and feel divine.

I had just slipped my shorts on when I notice something on the bathroom window sill. A piece of paper. Narrowing my eyes at it, I consider leaving it alone. That would be the decent thing to do.

Too bad I'm not decent.

The paper is slightly damp from the steam. It wasn't here before. I know that for a fact, since I closed the exact window it was leaning against before I had my shower. It makes me nervous to think about how it got there. No one would have gotten in without me noticing. Unless, of course, I had fallen into such a state of bliss I didn't notice an intruder.

I unfold it. This is for me, most definitely. Who else would have a note addressed to them from Fate himself?

I believe you have an obligation to fulfil.

Sinful and I are waiting.

And neither of us are very patient.

Fate

Fine hairs on the back of my neck stand up. I knew what obligations he was speaking of. This Sinful man, who I hope I never have to meet, wants Rylan to sin. But Rylan explained his belief to me, and how he wanted to wait until the ceremony.

Ever since I got sick, our relationship has gone on the backburner. Kaden hasn't relented in his pursuit for me. Fate is trying to lure me into a backdoor deal. Everything seems to be fighting us off. What Rylan and I need is time alone if we are going to make this work. Part of me wants to escape, but another part can't ignore how good I feel next to my mate.

I can tell Rylan is itching to prove it to me. He wants this over, so maybe we can have a chance. Spending the rest of my life with him is daunting, but at the same, it's starting to plant itself as normal in my mind.

I drop the note and fall to the toilet, throwing up promptly.

By the time I'm finished, I feel weak and my body trembles. Flushing the toilet, I push away, laying back on the cool tiles. The feeling eats at the fever that is tempted to consume my entire body.

It seems I'm not going to live much longer, anyway. I'm not sure what I'm stressing myself out about.

I throw Fate's note out the window, whispering good riddance after him. Then, I brush my teeth thoroughly. I don't want Rylan to figure out I'm sick like this again. I don't want to worry him...

Rylan is awake and pulling a fresh shirt over his head when I walk out. We meet gazes silently. I doubt he has any clue of how touchy he tends to be in slumber. My body still burns with the memory of his arms around me. They only intimacy I have had in a long time has been hugging Lucy close at night for warmth in the forest. The desire pack was the last time I was ever touched by a male.

"Good morning," he murmurs. His eyes, deliberately or not, fall down my body, gracing my legs, hips and breasts with his gaze. When my eyes get his full attention again, a slight blush tints his cheeks, and he turns away.

I grin knowingly, glad he was looking.

Rylan's shy side is one I quite enjoy seeing surface. He doesn't show it all that often, trying to hide it behind an indifferent facade. Fate's note plays in my mind, but I try to shun the memory. It will take a lot more convincing to get me to corrupt his religion. Some things I can't do, even if I don't have much control of my body right now.

"Do you know when Thea is arriving?" I ask, leaning back against the wall as I watch Rylan curiously.

He's refusing to look at me, which gives me great pleasure. I wonder if he realizes that when he acts like this, I know *exactly* what is wrong. He's trying to keep the thoughts out of his head; the same that I let flow through mine. If I didn't admit I'm devastatingly attracted to Rylan, I would burst from frustration. Yet at the same time, I can't get caught up over it, otherwise I will go into my heat.

I watch Rylan's shoulders while he shrugs, "I'm not sure, Dawn."

"I feel better," I muse. Yeah, after a shower.

The silence stretches between us. I'm not exactly sure what Rylan is doing, facing his back to me like that. From what I

125

assume, he's pretending to look at something on the dresser to take his attention from me. Honestly, I don't mind though. It's the best for both of us, I believe.

"I'm glad," I barely hear Rylan say. "That's all I want."

"Is it?"

There is more silence. This time, though, it's marginally different. The air between us is so thick with tension that I can hardly move. Instead, I just embrace it, waiting for Rylan to turn around and do something. *Anything.*

He does turn around, pinning me with his eyes as he does so. An expression I'm not used to seeing drenches his face. Is that... lust?

We stare at each other for a few seconds before Rylan advances on me.

His entire demeanour instantly changes. He looks suddenly confident and sure of himself; his shoulders straighten back. His eyes, once warm and familiar, are dark and tempting, looking awfully too sinful for a man of purity. My heart stops at the sight of him. Something has snapped in him, and it isn't about to repair itself.

His hands are on the sides of my shoulders very suddenly, his face close to mine. The man in front of me isn't the Rylan I despised in the forest. It's not the kind-hearted Rylan I've begun to like either. It's an alluring, seductive man that my body desperately wants.

"Rylan ..." I breathe, confusion fighting against the temptation of my mate in front of me.

He doesn't waste his time listening to me. Instead, he bends down, his lips on mine in a very insistent kiss. It's hungry, it's raw, and it hurts. It hurts to hold myself back, feeling the heat of his lips and the taste of his tongue. His hands on the wall are a delightful trap as he ravishes me, drawing out a part of me I've kept hidden for a long time.

If he keeps kissing me like this, he won't be any kind of alpha of purity ever again. Especially in the way he's touching me now; his hands on my waist and hips.

"Rylan," I repeat breathlessly, the pleasure of his lips transferring to my jaw, and down my neck. "This is wrong."

He makes a noise of irritation against my neck, ignoring me as he draws his tongue across my skin, his teeth scraping my neck hungrily. I would question what he was doing if I wasn't so desperate to dig my hands in his hair and pull him closer, wanting to feel the entire expanse of his body against mine forever.

"Ry ... what are you doing?" I gasp out, his fingers squeezing my waist very suddenly.

He pulls away, allowing me only seconds of his gaze as he forces out, "I'm losing control."

There was no hope for my reply, which was stolen away with his lips on mine.

Chapter Twenty-Two

Dawn

A sense of dread I've never felt before is draped over me.

I haven't seen those golden eyes of desire for three years. When I knew Asher, we were both young and stupid, before he was announced as Aapha. He had roped me in with the charming words he'd spun, and his addictive touch. Our kind of, but not really, relationship that we'd established was mutually beneficial for both of us, however, there was nothing like love there.

He's part of the reason why mother decided we should move away from the desire pack. To save me from the temptations of boys like him.

He's not a boy anymore. He's grown up, and almost a completely different person.

No one else seems to notice the tension between us, as Rylan stands, walking over to Asher to shake his hand. He has no idea. At least I hope he has no idea. Rylan doesn't even flinch, as Asher's gaze remains on mine for a good second, radiating with a fierce, uncompromising intelligence. Knowing. Then he drags that gaze to Rylan and he smiles lazily.

Glancing out the window, I wonder how much force it would take for me to make it through and plummet to my death, just to escape this situation.

"So great to see you, Alpha," Asher says smoothly, shaking hands with Rylan while patting the side of his arm warmly. I can hardly see the relationship between the two. One of desire, the other of purity. Their stark differences would suggest hostility between the two, however, they look rather warm toward each other.

As Rylan turns back to me, I catch Asher's gaze again. He has those bedroom eyes; his dark hair falling into them.

His wink is subtle, as he bites the edge of his lip through a knowing smile, before he turns and follows Alden toward the edge of the room. His gaze is smooth as he saunters away, while I glower at his back. He wears a dark jacket, the gold thread curling across the back into the symbol of allegiance to his pack. The golden wolf.

Rylan sits next to me, stealing my attention. He smiles at me, not suspecting a thing.

"So, it's sorted then," Thea says, clapping her hands together. Jasper has stood to join Alden and Asher. It's unnerving being in the same room as so many alphas. Potentially volatile and dangerous.

I remind myself not to mention my past 'relationship' with Asher to Rylan.

"I guess," I murmur distractedly, running my hand back through my hair. It takes all my focus to not flit my gaze over to the alpha of desire. He could say anything right now; do anything. "I'm going to die either way, right?"

Thea looks grim. "I had the same mentality. It's different though. It was my mate bringing me back."

"You'll be fine," Rylan reminds me softly, resting his hand on my knee. The movement, to him, is innocent, however, my entire body tenses up. My mind plummets to a dark place that last surfaced when Rylan spontaneously kissed me, and for a moment, I considered it the fault of Asher's presence.

Thea, struggling to stand with the size of her stomach, took my attention away as Rylan stood to help her up. I followed them toward Asher and Alden, who stood close to the kitchen, discussing something.

Asher looked up as I walked closer. His gaze is deliberate as it sears down my body, as conspiratorial as a wink. I notice a shadow pass over his eyes, which I pray Rylan didn't notice.

"Asher and I are going downtown later tonight, if any of you are interested in joining us," Alden offers smoothly, passing his gaze evenly between us.

Jasper shakes his head. "I better stay back with my very pregnant mate."

Thea gives him a stern look, which he smiles at.

"I'll have to stay back with mine too, while she isn't well," Rylan explains, as if Alden - the alpha of wisdom - didn't understand. Perhaps he did see the recognition in Asher's eyes when he first saw me. "The mate bond might be the only thing keeping her from throwing up, so I don't think we will be going anywhere."

I cast my gaze down, as I hear Asher chuckle, before saying, "Making us feel bad for not having a mate, alphas?"

"Time will tell," Jasper replies simply, as if one of us here believes in anything but Fate.

Thea grabs my arm, forcing my attention back to her. The males carried on speaking between each other, bantering about mates and a lack thereof. If Thea wasn't here, I would have tried to make an escape right now, just when I thought I wouldn't bother anymore.

"I know this will sound weird," Thea begins, "but would tomorrow be okay for your ... death? Jasper and I have to get back to our pack."

"Of course," I say uneasily. Not an easy thing to grasp my mind around, but I have little choice in the matter.

Once Rylan had finished discussing things with the other alphas, Alden decided I needed further rest, and Rylan happily obliged his request, leading my by the arm back to the bedroom. I followed, grateful to split the tension between Rylan, Asher and I.

"I'm going to die tomorrow," I say as we walk into the room, Rylan closes the door slowly behind him. "Kaden's going to get what he wants."

Rylan chuckles, saying, "You're going to come back, don't worry. Jasper knows what he's doing."

If there's anything to trust, it's Jasper. He's the oldest alpha out of all of them, and matches Alden in a lot of his wisdom. Alden has raw intelligence though, while Jasper's knowledge comes with all his centuries of life experience. Obviously though, I'm terrified. How could I not be? My mind won't cease with the thoughts of what could go wrong until it actually happens.

"Remember what I said about looking after Lucy if anything happens to me," I remind him, which he frowns at. "And please, look after yourself."

The idea of Lucy being without me is terrifying, and so is Rylan being without me. I've heard stories of mates killing themselves after the other dies, and I may have once wished it upon him, but now it hurts to imagine him in pain. He seems to realize my intentions as his expression softens and he walks toward me, cupping my face gently.

"Nothing is going to happen to you," he reassures me, as if I can't hear the doubt in his voice. I relax into his touch, feeling the aching headache forming in my temples begin to subside. Only the touch of a mate can do that.

"Remember our promise though, even if it applies sometime later in our lives," I repeat, trying to get it through to him how important this is to me.

He leans forward and kisses my forehead twice, then my cheek three times and pulls away with a bright smile on his face. He shakes his head at me in wonder. "What do I have to do to convince you everything is okay and will be okay?"

"Tell me I'm not going to die tomorrow. Tell me Kaden doesn't want me dead."

Something flickers in his eye. Pity or guilt? It passes within a second.

131

"Trust me," he says firmly. "Trust me in whatever happens, because all I want to do is protect you."

I didn't question his words. Instead, we lay down together to rest. By the time I next woke up, it was dark outside, and Rylan was still slumbering beside me peacefully. I slid out of bed, feeling wide-awake in an instant.

The window shows the vast night of the wisdom pack. Twinkling lights like stars decorate my vision as they reach from the buildings near us all the way to the horizon. I take a moment to admire them, remembering the nights I would sit on the perimeter wall of the purity pack, looking over the pack, grateful for never being in the hands of Rylan.

When I glance over my shoulder, I remember the promise to compromise.

I also remember what it was like to be free.

Sighing, I wander out the bedroom, and down the hall, caught in thought. If I had never gotten sick, or been threatened by Kaden, I would be in the Freedom Pack, living a basic life. I'd live where I wouldn't or didn't have to die and become a phantom wolf, or worry about Fate wanting me to seduce Rylan into sinning. Right now, it's almost impossible to think of a simpler life like that.

I'm suddenly jerked out of thought, as I walk into the kitchen, feet padding against the linoleum.

Asher is standing under a small light, shirtless and sipping from a glass of water. We meet gazes for a good moment, before he smiles, chuckling slightly.

"Alpha of purity, huh Dawn? Would have never thought *you* to be the one. Or should I say, *his* one," Asher teases, and I narrow my eyes on him.

Making sure I'm not too close, I rest against the bench closest to me. "Fate, right?"

He shrugs loosely. He never used to be this attractive. I remember when he was the awkward teenager, with the short cropped hair and gangly body. He looks as though he's been to hell and back, and seen something I would never understand, and has

132

decided to change almost everything about himself, aside from those brilliant golden eyes and dark hair, which nearly falls into his eyes now.

He's gained a significant amount of muscle on his torso, which I can't help but notice with his lack of shirt. Now that he's an alpha, he also seems to have gotten taller, more handsome, and a lot more arrogant, considering the confident gazes and winks he's been giving me since he arrived.

"So, what has Dawn been doing these past few years?" Asher asks, as if he cares. If anything, he wants to bring up our history just to embarrass me, or maybe to draw out a reaction from Rylan.

He's like that. Manipulative, teasing ... seductive.

That's how I got roped into his bed the first time. It was a stupid mistake that I made him aware of after the first... I can't remember how many times.

"Living my life away from the desire pack," I say flatly, watching him as he slowly take a sip of his water. I've found the water here tastes too much like chemicals. "Which I suppose you have been leading. How's that been going for you?"

Asher raises an eyebrow. "Brilliantly."

The silence between us is something I take great solitude in. I contemplate turning around to walk away, until he spoke again.

"I miss you," he murmurs.

"No you don't."

He smirked, setting his glass down slowly beside him. His sudden steps toward me take me by surprise, as I keep myself against the bench, feeling the cool marble through the back of my shirt. Asher's voice is as soft as honey as he says, "I miss very specific parts of you, Dawn."

I hate the way he says my name like that. "I should really be heading back to bed."

"Come on, where's the fun girl I used to know?" he questions, coming so close I'm left considering what he's about to do next. He leans in, his mouth by my ear. "Or hasn't your mate roughed you up yet?"

I push at his chest, but he doesn't budge. "You're lucky, Asher, that my illness isn't contagious to alphas, because I would find great pleasure in being the one to kill *you*."

His brow furrows, but he passes his confusion off.

"You're lucky, Dawn, that I have restraint, because right now, you're looking awfully delicious-"

A cleared throat makes me suddenly jump, as I turn my head, meeting the gaze of my mate.

Chapter Twenty-Three

Dawn

Asher didn't move back, despite Rylan's presence.

He knew he was there. How long my mate had been watching I don't know, but something told me Asher was fully aware of it the entire time. He's like that. He enjoys getting a rise out of people and seeing them react. The real tip-off that he knew was the smirk that continued to play on his lips, as he looked down at me, not bothering to acknowledge Rylan.

"What's going on?" Rylan asks softly, sounding lost, distant.

The silence is deadly, before Asher chuckles, his golden eyes gleaming as he says, "Dawn and I were just catching up on things. It's been a while since her and I talked, Rylan. I can promise you nothing else is going on."

Asher didn't sound convincing on any level. He had no interest in continuing the conversation between us, or at the very least, in preserving the respect between him and the alpha of purity. At this point, I knew he'd say anything to rile him, especially since I was the one who was going to have to do the explaining.

I risk a glance back up at Rylan. His expression is painted in indifference, but I notice the way his hand clenches the edge of the archway.

"Dawn is sick, Asher. She shouldn't be awake right now," Rylan says bluntly.

I bite the edge of my lip, stopping myself from arguing back at him. The way he didn't address me with that statement is... infuriating. Asher doesn't seem fazed at all, however, he finally pushes back, leaving a decent space between us so I can finally breathe.

"Perhaps we will have time to really talk tomorrow, Dawn," Asher says, quirking an eyebrow up at me before he turns to Rylan and says, "You may have your mate back, Alpha."

And with that said, Asher brushed past Rylan, and left the kitchen.

Rylan watches me silently, clearly debating what to say as much as I am. This is the first time I've seen him act like this. I'm not even sure *what* he is acting like. This silent admission to the mate bond would be amusing to me, on another day, but I saw the look in his eyes when he caught us. It made me feel as if Asher had turned me around and bent me over the kitchen bench, even though it was a simple exchange of words, nothing more.

"That didn't sound so innocent," he says finally, and I exhale slowly. He had heard. *Great.*

"I'm tired," I say flatly. Striding towards the kitchen exit, I'm stopped by Rylan, who grabs my arm tightly. My jaw clenches, before I look up at him. "I don't want to talk about it right now."

Rylan shakes his head at me, practically seething, as he says, "I won't be able to sleep until I get an explanation."

I look over my shoulder. The rest of Alden's open-plan apartment is empty, of course, but it still makes me nervous talking about this. So, grabbing Rylan's arm, I lead him back to our room. Luckily, he didn't protest at this.

Rylan walks into the room, and I close the door securely behind him. When I turn back to look at him, he has a serious expression painted on his face. He even has his arms folded over his awfully... bare... chest. I swallow, bringing my eyes back to his eyes, which are full of a gentle blue moonlight.

I take that back. An *angry* moonlight.

"Asher and I knew each other before I left the desire pack - before he even became alpha," I tell Rylan, keeping my back against the door while he stands close to the bed. I'll let him seethe far away from me.

"I figured," he said slowly. "I assume there was more between you than what you are implying."

I sigh, before I say, "We ... shared a bed a few times, but I promise you it was nothing more than that. You know what he's like; he was just trying to mess with you tonight. He's a tease, a manipulator."

My words don't seem to be making a difference to the mask of irritation that was evident across his face. It can't be nice to hear your mate was involved with another alpha before you, but I didn't know what else to say. I couldn't have lied and told him Alpha Asher is just a hopeless flirt and he and I had no history.

Slowly, Rylan sat down on the side of the bed, and my heart fell.

"Are you mad?" I ask softly, testing the waters. Rylan gets mad quickly, and easily, for an alpha of purity. I remember when he threw the glass over my head and at the wall. I make a mental reminder to talk to him about that in the future.

"I shouldn't be," he murmurs, looking up at me beneath strands of his hair which are as lustrous as onyx stone. "But I can't deny that the thought of you with *him* makes me furious."

I'm quick to sit beside him, not at all afraid of him and his potential anger. If I had heard about a sexual relationship that he'd had with another girl, I would be upset too. I suppose it's a mate thing, although now, the thought of any other male near me that isn't Rylan in a suggestive manner makes me feel ill, and not because I'm sick. *That's* how I know the mate bond is setting deeper in stone.

"Past is the past, right?" I say, nudging him gently. He turns to look at me. He knows what I mean by that. That I'm trying to put the year and a half I spent running from him in the past, as hard as it might seem to be.

137

The adamant expression he had built finally cracked with the slight hint of a smile. I wrapped my arm around his shoulder and kissed his cheek, before sliding back onto the bed; my back hitting the headboard. Rylan stays on the edge of the bed, shoulders slumped. I don't make another move, just staring at his back, wishing I could read his mind.

"I love you," he says suddenly.

I pause, my heart stopping with my entire body. I didn't know what to say for a moment, until Rylan spoke again.

"I don't expect you to share the feeling right now, but I know for a fact that it is real. I truly do love you," he continues, his voice honey-soft and vulnerable.

I close my eyes, just as I hear Rylan stand and walk to the wall to switch the light off.

***

"Okay, maybe I changed my mind about this," I say slowly, eyeing the needle in Jasper's hand. It's making me increasingly nervous knowing what the blue liquid in the syringe meant. Death. That's what.

Thea is on one side, while Rylan is on the other. Thea is calm and subdued, making sure Jasper knew what to do, while Alden stood at the doorway, correcting her on some things. Rylan held my hand tightly as I lay back, looking down at me. He's trying his hardest to hide his doubt, however, I can still see it. I'm mirroring it, I'm sure.

"It's going to be fine," Thea assures me by my ear. "I promise you."

I have no choice. Unless I want to be pinned by Rylan's side to try mitigate the pain this fast-acting disease has on me, I have to do this. What I'm most terrified about, though, isn't the dying. It's the creature I will be when I wake up again.

Jasper told me as much as he could about being a phantom wolf. A part of me has been too scared to fully acknowledge it. He's explained that I won't be able to get pregnant again, which I was the most disgusted by. It was my death that Alden warned would be nearing that made Rylan snap out of it, and finally agree.

"You'll all be here when I wake up?" I ask. It's the seventh time I've asked that. I don't know what I would do if I were to go through this alone.

"Of course," Rylan says softly, brushing my hair back with his fingers. "We will all be right here, after Jasper does his... thing."

Bite me. That's what.

"You won't feel any of it, I promise," Thea says. The way she keeps repeating the word 'promise' makes me nervous. She is trying to convince me that this will be okay, so I won't back out at the last minute.

"Are you ready?" Jasper suddenly asks, making me jump. My hand clenches Rylan's tightly, as Thea moves so Jasper can stand by me instead.

He looks bothered by this all. I was told he was the one who had to take Thea's life to turn her into a phantom wolf, which wouldn't have been easy on him, considering she's his mate. It would completely change Rylan if he had to do that to me.

"I guess," I whisper, the nerves I knew were to come were finally creeping into my veins. Am I really doing this?

I have to, there's no other choice.

I look away when Jasper slides the needle into my skin. Rylan held my gaze, and at that moment, I truly saw the love he had for me. It's real.

Drowsiness was quick to follow the sting of the needle. Rylan stooped down, holding my chilled hands in his warm ones. He suddenly looked frantic, knowing it's too late to take back the poison that is now streaming through my veins and going straight to my heart.

It's his final words to me that send a chill down my spine. "Whatever happens, trust me."

I would have questioned, but as if a switch had been flicked, my eyes drifted closed, and I fell into unconsciousness.

***

Nothing hurt when I woke. My entire body was at peace with itself, as I lay there, drifting on a cloud.

Then I realized.

Sitting up, my eyes fly open. I'm fine. I'm not sick. And what's especially important is that I'm not dead. The turning must have been successful.

The sense of optimism was stolen, as I noticed someone at the foot of my bed, which is hardly familiar. But there the eyes are; cold and cruel. Kaden stared down at me, an eyebrow raised as he watched me with a sense of victory.

Then the worst happened.

The door to the room opened, and in walked Rylan. My mate. With the sickest and most sadistic smile on his face.

Chapter Twenty-Four

Dawn

"Someone better explain to me what the hell is going on."

It's not Kaden's expression that has me worried. He can look as conspiratorial and as evil as he wants, and it wouldn't surprise me. But Rylan? I'm staring into the blank, vacant eyes of a male I don't recognise, that devilish smile on his face so disturbing. It's the kind of smile that admits to the sins I never knew he committed.

Kaden shrugs loosely. He doesn't care as he says, "I think I'll give your mate the honor of explaining."

I snap my gaze to Rylan. He's looking at Kaden ... fondly. The sight makes me feel sick, betrayed, and not because I've just woken up from death itself. Rylan hates Kaden. Kaden hates me. It was an even circle of hatred that has turned into one thing.

Me hating both of them.

"You're looking decent," Rylan says, dragging a heavy gaze down my body. It's almost offending. I've seen him do it shyly before, embarrassed that I caught him admiring me. Now, he seems pleased, even arrogant. It's a look I wouldn't mind slapping off him. But I won't until I get an answer out of him. "For someone who died."

I can imagine I hardly look decent, but I keep my mouth shut in that regard, deciding instead to say, "That's not an answer, Rylan."

Kaden sighs, clapping his hands together. The sound vibrates throughout the room I had been too busy to notice. I'm on a small mattress with no sheets; a metal frame is the only thing keeping me up. Beyond it are slick concrete floors that meet the walls of this small room. It looks like a prison without the bars.

"You're in my pack now. And before you ask, no, I'm not going to kill you, as tempting as it may be," Kaden informs me. I glance at Rylan for a reaction, but he looks indifferent, his smile gone. Instead, he tilts his head at me, regarding me in a way that arises nerves within me.

"The vengeance pack." I breathe. "Why?"

Kaden looks at Rylan pointedly, throwing the conversation over to him. I follow his gaze, narrowing my eyes at him in expectation.

"Because we brought you here," Rylan tells me. I respond a growl. "We decided that this was the perfect time to smuggle you out of the purity pack without anyone noticing my absence for too long."

Finally, a proper, functional sentence out of his mouth, but I'm not sure how much I would like to hear now. That stubborn streak within me has decided I want out of here, away from Rylan... if that's even who he really is. Perhaps I woke up in an alternate universe where Rylan is a crazed killer and Kaden is a little angel. It sure looks that way.

I look at Kaden, and I see a relaxed man. He's in his own pack, with his mate again. Suddenly, he has no reasons for games or riddles. If he wanted me dead, I would be dead. That's the confusing part.

But Rylan? He's completely baffled me.

I go to breeze past the two, happy to leave this place without a second thought. It's foolish, of course, as Kaden grabs my arm, pulling me back, so I'm evenly spaced between both him and Rylan. They look down at me with unreadable expressions.

"You're not going anywhere, Dawn," Kaden says coolly. I rip away from him, taking a step back again.

It's strange how my body has reacted to the transformation. I feel brilliant, as if I've slept a decent amount and woken up to a sunny day outside. There's something new though. A spring to my

142

step, maybe? A buzz that tingles and dances across my skin to my fingertips. I'm not average anymore. I'm a Phantom. I'm technically dead, yet at the same time, so alive.

"I would like answers," I snap, before adding with less hostility, "and a look in the mirror. I was told I would inherit Jasper's eye color."

Rylan's own eyes gleam. "I can assure you that's not an incorrect fact."

"Answers..."

Kaden sighs again. He's good at that, as if he's always lacking patience around us. He then nods to the door, and starts making his way over, mumbling something about how he was going to give us space to figure things out. I watched the door closed behind him before I turned and slapped Rylan straight across the face.

His face snaps back in response. The first reaction from him is an amused chuckle, and a smirk to match. He looks back at me; an unfamiliar fire in his eyes.

"You want me to say sorry?"

"I thought that was a given," I growl, utterly frustrated at his change in attitude. I spent a long time trying to figure out the Rylan who was there before I was killed by Jasper. I'm not sure how I feel about this new one.

"A given?"

"Like you wouldn't believe, you dirty, filthy, disgusting liar."

Rylan folds his arms against chest, in what I assume is a mocking gesture. He looks awfully smug, as if he's enjoying my anger, my discomfort. It's sign number one that Kaden has messed with his head.

"I never lied to you," Rylan says calmly. I'm surprised at his audacity.

"You dragged me into the vengeance pack, where my enemy resides. Kaden wants me dead... does that not register in your mind? You never consulted with me in *anything* and now you're speaking as if you're Kaden creating a riddle. Do you work for

143

him? I also want to add how you seem to have completely changed personalities-"

All of a sudden, I'm cut off as Rylan makes a single stride toward me, grabbing my face with a rough, surprising grip as he presses his lips against mine.

I'm shocked for a moment, the kiss rough and raw and unlike anything I would expect from Rylan. He runs his tongue across the seam of my lips, as if I would accept the heat of this kiss, and somehow return his affection. Instead, I push him violently away, the force enough to send him back a few steps. He's grinning like the arrogant pig he's turned into.

"I took you from the purity pack, which has been your wish for a long time, hasn't it?" Rylan asks, and I growl.

"Not to the vengeance pack."

"I helped us both escape," Rylan tells me, finally sobering up a little to take things seriously. "You see, as the alpha of the purity pack, I'm expected to be the puritan that prays to the moon goddess and believes my entire pack should too."

I swallow nervously. "You don't believe?"

"Hardly. The goddess has no power, Dawn, you know that. However, sticking to the tradition of my dead parents, I must pretend I'm the perfect alpha, to avoid mass hysteria. I wanted to get you out of that pack as soon as possible."

I take a moment to understand his words. Instead, I shake my head, adding another question to the mix. "Why would I need to escape? Is it because I'm the worst possible influence as a luna, because I can't say right now that you're a stand-up alpha."

"I'm currently working on a way to remedy the situation," Rylan tells me. This doesn't sound good....

I raise an eyebrow. "Explain."

"The purity pack runs off the belief that the moon goddess decides their entire lives, and without that system, these people would go crazy," Rylan tells me, as if I'm not aware. "A few years ago, the goddess lost all her power to Fate, and left to live her life

144

as normal. Any sense that she no longer has power won't be accepted, which is why you can't be in that pack."

In other words, he doesn't want them to see me as a luna, because everyone will figure out my doubt for their beliefs.

"You don't seem to be much of a saint anymore," I proclaim, folding my arms across my chest like he has, adding, "Lying is a sin."

"I never lied. I simply kept this from you for the better, so no one could know we took you here. Your death sufficed as a perfect cover up to sneak you out of the wisdom pack without any complications," Rylan explained.

I wanted to ask about Kaden. About his role in this, but I couldn't bear to mention his name right now. Something else was on my mind.

"Why didn't you ever tell me?" I ask; my voice croaky and broken unintentionally.

A year ago, I couldn't imagine a way that Rylan could betray me. That would mean never trusting him... but he had been so kind. He looked after me, and I felt myself beginning to fall for the male, liking his calm, soft personality. At this revelation, my heart ached with more pain than any physical wound could potentially inflict. I have just enough strength not to fall to the floor by his feet and cry.

"It was better, the less I explained. We couldn't have any complications in getting you out," Rylan tells me. He's not apologetic in any sense. He's flat, impassive and infuriating.

I exhale shakily. "The Rylan I thought I knew wouldn't even consider this, but I suppose that was an act."

Rylan nodded smoothly, and my heart broke a little more.

"So, if you're not religious, then the ceremony shouldn't have mattered. Sinning shouldn't worry you-"

"Oh, don't worry," Rylan says, cutting me off, "I have no problem with sinning. I've done it multiple times before."

Rylan may have taken my flinch for one of surprise on his part. Sure, hearing this was shocking, but my mind wandered elsewhere.

145

To Fate. He lied. He told me Sinful wanted me to seduce Rylan into sinning, but if he already has…?

"I've killed before," Rylan tells me.

Again, I flinch.

"I've had sex before," he continues.

I refuse to react to that one.

He takes step forward, recovering the ones he lost when I pushed him away. His eyes are bright with mischief that I despise.

"What did you do to the Rylan I know?" I question, my voice soft.

Rylan's finger comes under my chin as he lifts it, smiling triumphantly as he says, "He never existed."

Chapter Twenty-Five

Rylan

The way Dawn looked at me. So hurt.

I thought I finally had her. Before this revelation, I fully believed Dawn had accepted a life with me and wanted to try, and not just for Lucy, her sister. Now, I can see the disdain in her eyes, as she regards me, probably contemplating ways to either kill me or escape.

"I just don't understand why ... why Kaden?" she questions, her voice hoarse as if she's attempting to hide back tears. I don't think I could handle it if she let them fall.

I can't stand here and pretend to be the man back in the purity pack. He's someone I should be. He wants to do good for all in his pack, believing with them in the goddess. Of course, I'm not him. Not anymore. That year without Dawn killed me. It crushed the good part of my heart while I was at my worst, wondering why my mate didn't want me.

"He helped me find you," I tell her. I wish it was easy to explain the situation. She never wanted me, but I *needed* her. Not just so my pack would have a luna - which was my excuse to Kaden - but because she's my mate.

Someone I have been waiting for my entire life.

"In return," I continue, "I have to help him. Luckily, he has allowed us to stay here, so you can know the truth."

"Why couldn't I have known before?" she questions, although her tone is closest to a growl. From the short time I have known Dawn, I have decided she doesn't like being frustrated. She would rather be out, running around and free with her mind and her body. I wish I could give her that... If I let her out for a single second, though, she would be out of here. Especially after this revelation.

I sigh before I answer, "People listen. Servants listen. If any of them had any doubts about my beliefs, I would have lost everything."

She seems to actually understand that and doesn't retaliate against me.

"Do you actually want to be my mate?" she questions carefully. "Did you mean it when you told me you love me?"

She didn't meet my eyes as she said that, which ripped away at my heart. She's the main reason I changed. I didn't want her to know that. I told her it because of my religion that I'm like that, but that isn't the full truth. What if she thinks I'm a weak alpha because being without her almost killed me? I've tried all along to seem strong in that regard in front of her.

"Of course I love you," I say softly, "you're my mate, and that will never change."

I'm not sure if she believed me, which gave me the worst feeling in the world. Yet I couldn't find any more words to say that would change things. I don't blame her for wanting to get away from me for an entire year... Normal girls don't have to worry about someone like me.

She may not believe in the religion of my pack, but I bet she would consider any one of them after what I put here through. No, I did it for her.

She veered straight off the topic suddenly, saying, "What do you owe Kaden?"

"He has been working on getting the moon goddess's powers back, after they were taken by Fate. If that happens, she will be able to restore her power to her religion, which has been what she

148

has wanted for quite some time. I'm sure she would explain better to you, as to why she changed her mind," I explain.

Dawn takes a moment to think that through, her eyebrows furrowing in that way I have always admired.

"Why would Kaden want to help anyone?" she asks.

"For his mate, who was a purity Ppack member, and for his daughter," I tell her. She doesn't yet know about the real Kaden. The one who has a life outside of the ruthless, merciless killing he has been involved with in the past.

Dawn takes a seat back on the bed, clearly trying to make sense of everything. At the same time as expecting her to want to leave, and having to give her that want, I hope she doesn't. Once Millicent, the moon goddess, has her powers restored, life might go back to the normal. Dawn, however, seems to be battling with an internal conflict.

Then she looks up at me with wild eyes.

"I might be able to help with that."

***

Dawn

I'm not sure how I should summon fate, exactly.

I have spent a great amount of time trying not to think of him, or listen to his prompts to make Rylan sin. It seems weird to want to get him here now.

I refuse to tell Rylan about my plan. He might ruin it. I have questions for Fate right now anyway, so whether I can convince him to give some of his power-up, which is slim, or not, I want to know why he wanted Rylan to sin. My mate had told me to my face that he had had sex before, which has confused me beyond belief.

I've decided to summon Fate into the room I have been allocated. I'm surprised that it has a window. I would think Rylan wouldn't want me to escape in the night and try get over the wall

149

that keeps people in the vengeance pack. Then again, this pack was created to keep prisoners in. I would just like to get back to the purity pack to get Lucy.... Who's looking after that poor girl right now?

I sit down on the edge of the bed. I'm grateful Rylan didn't demand I share a room with him. I think he's worried I might shift into a phantom wolf into the night.

Apparently that's going to happen soon.

"Okay ..." I say into the air, gripping the edges of the duvet under me. It's made of a strange feeling fabric I'm not used to. "Fate, I'm not sure where you are, but I kind of need you here right now."

Silence. No answer to the thought-phone I was ringing through to. Does he even hear my words? Or is this just a strange assumption I have made-

"Good evening, Dawn."

I look up from where I was staring at the floor. Clambering through the window, was Fate. He'd dressed in his same dark jacket and pants, the shirt underneath being the same ebony color. I'm not sure what it is with him and well-fitting black outfits like that. They make his bright hair stand out when against his features and endless obsidian eyes. I'm yet to ask why he has hair like that.

I place my hand over my heart. "Thank you for scaring the hell out of me."

"You did call," Fate adds, as the window slides magically closed behind him. I watch the movement, suddenly doubting calling him to me. He could do anything he pleases, and I have no way to fight back.

"We need to talk...."

Fate stands in front of me, smirking slightly. "Naturally. I see you're in the vengeance pack after all. Your mate finally decided to tell you."

"Rylan has sinned. Why did you lie? What would you and Sinful get out of me sleeping with Rylan before the ceremony I

150

assume he doesn't want anything to do with? I'm hoping you have the decency to tell me the truth this time, because I'm really sick of being lied to," I snap.

Fate looks a little surprised, before his smile resumes. "I've always admired your backbone."

My fingers tap impatiently against the bed.

"Sinful simply wanted to expose Rylan to his pack and make them think he's not indebted to his religion. If one of his servants found out, it would spread like wildfire," Fate explains.

Something that makes a little sense, finally.

"What does Sinful have against Rylan?" I decide to ask.

At this point, Fate is wandering around the room, looking around. There isn't anything interesting in here. My belongings are supposed to be secretly taken from the pack later, so right now, I have nothing to speak of. Fate must be filling the space between our conversation, making me more frustrated at the lack of information.

"Nothing in particular," he muses, "he just enjoys messing with people, like me."

"I need your help," I say suddenly.

Fate's attention is on me in an instant. His eyebrow quirks up, clearly intrigued at my change of tone and urgency. I want to lay it all on the table for him to shut down quickly, so he can get out of here and leave me alone. Perhaps I should be less obvious about how much he intimidates me next time…

"Would you be willing to give the moon goddess some of her power back, for her-"

He holds his hand up, "I'm aware, although it is amusing watching you attempt to explain, looking as though you're going to pass out from fear of retaliation."

My expression drops, as I add, "How did you know?"

He chuckles. That sound makes me feel foolish. He's Fate, of course he knows. He probably knows what I had for breakfast this morning, or lack thereof, should I say.

151

"I am willing to give the moon goddess some of her power, on two conditions. I'm sure you will be willing to accept them if you would like to go back to the way things were before," Fate says, trying to water down whatever was to come next. Anything will be tempting at this point.

"Go on."

"Firstly, it would give me great amusement if the moon goddess would admit her love to her mate, who currently has no idea," Fate says. I frown, waiting for the second option before I spoke again.

"And the second ..." he drawls off.

A smile widens on his face, and shiver at the sight of it.

"It seems as though the mate bond between you and Rylan needs a little challenge," he says, and I instantly shake my head.

Fate holds his hand up again, silencing my protests.

"So, for the moon goddess's power, you will let me give you another mate, so I can ruffle Rylan's feathers, and let him work for it."

Chapter Twenty-Six

Dawn

"That's not an option."

There's a glint in Fate's eyes, as he regards me silently from across the room. He leant back against the wall, clearly getting bored since my last response took me a few minutes to muster. I had to weigh up everything. At the end of my line of thought, I had decided that there was no way that could ever happen.

Slowly, he stands. My hands clench on the bedsheets in response as I watch him carefully. I won't let any movement go unnoticed when he is posing an offer like this.

"What happened to the Dawn who took chances?" he asks, clasping his hands together as he raises a taunting eyebrow. "Was it Rylan who changed you, or did you do that to yourself? Although, I know who is responsible for your sister being left behind in the purity pack."

I tried not to let his words get to me. I *tried.*

"My sister won't benefit from me having another mate, I can assure you of that," I exclaim. If Fate hadn't meddled in Lucy's mind, she wouldn't want anything to do with Rylan, so I can't imagine how she would react to another mate of mine. I don't even know how I would react to that. One mate is surely enough. "I don't know a single person who would benefit from that aside from you."

"Exactly," he says cunningly. "It is me who is giving up some of my power, is it not? You can't expect me to rule anything out."

So manipulative... so Fate.

"You can't expect me to accept another mate. I don't even know why you would want that," I say, my voice calmer than the emotional turmoil currently going on inside my mind.

I've seen Rylan when he's angry. I've seen him when he's gotten jealous and protective. I highly doubt Fate has put that much effort into scrutinising that part of Rylan. Unless he has, which would explain his want to rile him up. Right now, that is the last thing I want to do, considering the current situation. Rylan could react in any way.

"That shouldn't matter. What matters, is I'll be getting what I am want, and you will be getting what you want, with a little extra on the side," Fate tells me, a conspiratorial smile gracing his features.

What I want. All I want is to be out of this entire mess and with my sister. Rylan has proved he can keep a secret a little too easily, and now, I'm left wondering what else he has up his sleeve. I didn't even know having another mate was even possible till now, and I can't imagine trying to explain that to Rylan either.

"Tell me who my mate would be," I decide to ask.

"That would take all the fun out of it," Fate muses, taking a few confident steps toward me, so that I flinch in response, "Wouldn't it?"

My eyes narrow at him. "I don't take myself and Rylan's personal suffering to be very fun."

Fate shakes his head at me, his closing strides toward me are ones I refuse to react to. My body is as frigid as a marble statue as he sits next to me, the bed sinking down with him. He smells strangely delightful, as if he's been walking through a forest at the crack of dawn. If sunlight and shadows together had a scent, he was wearing it.

"Your mate will be someone whose mate died many years ago," Fate continues, as if I hadn't spoken just before. "I might even be nice and let you choose who you would like to mark you in the end."

At those words, I push myself across the bed, away from him, saying, "You can't make me do that…"

"Alright, then I will make the decision for you."

I narrow my eyes and shake my head immediately. There is no way I would trust Fate with a decision that takes a little bit of heart and feeling. Can someone like him have a mate? Whoever got paired with someone like him, not only seems to be a jerk, but can manipulate your future with some of his power.

"Come on, take the deal," Fate prompts, his voice going softer suddenly, as if that will be what will convince me, "I promise that if you do, and the moon goddess admits her love to her mate, then everything will work out. You will have freedom again, and so will your sister. And you'll have a mate."

I know he is bringing up Lucy to tempt me. It's working. Of all people to mention, she's the one I'm doing this for. And Rylan too. He wants his pack back, and I don't blame him.

"There's no small little details in this deal that you will manipulate in the future?" I ask, although I don't expect the full truth. At this point, I am trying to convince myself into this, to save everyone, including the pack that is supposed to be mine too.

Fate chuckles. "I play my games fairly."

"Then I'll do it," I say, before every part of me wants to turn back.

***

Rylan could hardly believe I agreed to have another mate for the goddess's powers.

Mad didn't begin to describe it. Furious, maybe. Listening to his lectures on how I shouldn't sell myself to Fate, even for him, wasn't worth it, and that might have possibly been the worst decision I have ever made in my life. It took over an hour talking to him before he actually understood. To end the conversation, I reminded him that it was his decision that had left Lucy in the purity pack - even though he assured me she was looked after - and that I'm able to make a decision for myself.

Even though it's not the best one ...

I've spent the last few days in my room. Looking Kaden in the eye is more difficult than ever, and everyone else in this place is just like him. Except for his mate, Mara. She was a purity pack member before she mated him, with a mellow personality and a young daughter named Shaye, who I'm yet to decide which parent she resembled the best. She has Kaden's dark eyes and Mara's light hair.

The main reason I'm locked up in here is so I don't bump into my potential mate again. Rylan and I made that decision mutually, for once. Also, I don't want to face the consequences of being a murderer in the vengeance pack.

Where I belong, according to Kaden.

I'm laying down on the bed when there is a timid knock on the door. I know who it is immediately. Mara does this every day, and has done since I've gotten here.

"Come in."

The door opens, and Mara slides in, closing it after her quickly. She's without Shaye today, which is new. I'm used to the young girl sitting on the edge of my bed, playing around with toys Mara would bring with her. She's a great mum. She's soft and kind and the complete opposite to her mate. I'm not judging though. Rylan and I don't necessarily have much in common either.

"Just wanted to check on you," she says warmly. She's dressed in a bright flowery dress, which suits her, and the weather around us. "Rylan is worrying."

"I know, but he doesn't want me out of this room as much as I want to be. Could bump into my other mate, you know?" I say with an exhale of irritation.

Mara comes to sit on the bed with me, crossing her legs while keeping her dress pressed down. "I just want to tell you, because no one else has the guts to do it themselves, that what you did was really brave and admirable. If I had a sister, I would do the exact same thing."

I've come to the conclusion that Mara is the only decent person in this place. She has the prettiest blue eyes that are so full of light, it's mesmerizing. I'm jealous of her, and the life she seems so pleased with.

Why can't everything be so easy?

"I'm not sure about that. I've got a mate out there somewhere, who I could meet any time from now to when I die," I tell her. I've explained this a few times, but I don't think anyone really understands. How could they? Having two mates is completely unheard of, yet striking deals with Fate isn't.

"I'm sure Rylan hopes for the latter," Mara says jokingly, but her smile doesn't reach her eyes.

I glance down at where my hands are tracing across the thread of the duvet, keeping my mouth shut.

"You know, Rylan really does love you," Mara murmurs, catching my attention. Raising my gaze, I can see how sincere she looks. But she didn't see his face when I first woke up. She didn't see his face when he tied me down during these last few nights with silver chains, just in case I shifted into a phantom wolf that would kill everyone in this place.

So far, that hasn't happened.

"Perhaps you two should talk ... alone, about things," she offers.

"We have been alone-"

"To talk properly," she cuts in.

Sighing deeply, I slump back into the bed. When I look back at Mara, she is concentrating on her fingers knotted on her lap. She looks solemn, which isn't something I'm used to seeing as an expression on her face. I decide to question it, and with that, she takes a while to answer.

"Someone is coming here to visit tomorrow," she says quietly. "It is so out of the blue and unexpected...."

"Who?" I question, the hair on the back of my neck sticking up.

She bites the edge of her lip, before saying, "A friend of Kaden's from the discipline pack. All I can really say, is that we all think it's awfully convenient that he is coming to stay now, since Kaden hasn't seen him in quite some time."

I knew what she meant.

"So, you're saying, that you think that he might be my other mate?"

Chapter Twenty-Seven

Dawn

"I thought we agreed that you would stay in your room."

Rylan stands with his arms crossed over his chest, blocking the exit to my room. I shoot him a deadpan look. He knows very well that me staying in here for the rest of my life so I don't have to face the possibility of finding my other mate. I'm not even sure I would have any sense of mental stability after a few weeks.

Plus, I'm curious.

"You can't hide from your own fate, you know," I say, which Rylan understands very well, yet is still being stubborn. "He's going to come walking along one day and-"

"And I'll kill him."

I narrow my eyes at him. "Don't be like that."

He still doesn't move from where he stands. The man from the discipline pack that Mara mentioned has already arrived, and I'm curious to meet him. What if he is my other mate? How would *he* react to finding out he would be sharing with an alpha? Not thrilled, I'm sure. Especially since it is Fate's doing.

"The man is a bounty hunter that used to work for Kaden. He's no good anyway," Rylan comments, already knowing that is why I'm wanting to leave.

"Says you," I retort.

We stand there, staring each other down, both as stubborn as each other. At first, I didn't mind staying in here to get away from Kaden, who I doubt I will ever trust. Now, I'm begging him to let me out of this small room, even if it means still being locked up within Kaden's estate. I may hate him, but I must admit he has a lovely home, for the most part.

All of a sudden, the door opens behind Rylan. He turns to see who wanders in. She's strikingly familiar, and I flinch when I realize who she is.

One of Rylan's guards. The same one who had killed herself in the name of Kaden.

She seems to notice the looks I'm giving her, as I try fathom how exactly she is standing right in front of me, when I see Rylan's face. She says, "This is probably a strange sight. I'm sure Rylan has explained how it was necessary to pretend that Kaden was the bad guy, the entire time."

"Who are you?" I ask softly, as she wanders casually into the room past Rylan, stopping at my bed.

"My name is Milly," she replies, pulling the sheet forward as she begins to make my bed. "I used to be a prisoner here, but when I learned Kaden was not the despicable man I thought he was, I began working for him. My mission as Rylan's guard was my first ever outside one."

I had so many questions I wanted to ask her, but I kept my mouth shut. Whoever this Milly girl was, she was the perfect distraction for me to just... slip... past Rylan.

I barely make it past the bedroom door and into the corridor before Rylan halts me.

"Where do you think you're going?"

"To get myself some food," I reply. "I'm hungry."

Rylan follows tightly behind me as I make my way down the corridor. The only place I know how to get to here on my own is the main kitchen, which has become my friend late at night. So, I'm going to walk straight there, and if I happen to run into anyone on the way there, then so be it. Rylan can stand behind me all he wants.

There's no one in the kitchen when I walk in. I'm sure one of us is glad for that; the one who has gone strangely silent. It's not as if I'm specifically looking for that bounty hunter who has shown up here. I assume he's here with Kaden.

I'm also running off the belief that Mara was just assuming things. That he isn't actually my mate.

Rylan leans against the bench while I rummage through the fridge. I'm not sure what I'm looking for, but as long as I'm not looking back to match Rylan's scrutinizing gaze, I'm fine.

"You know, I would like to meet the moon goddess eventually."

"She goes by Millicent."

"That's useless to know if I never actually meet her," I retort, deciding that the only thing in the fridge I might like is an apple. I pull it out and turn around, facing Rylan. His arms are still over his chest, his gaze heavy with irritation.

I take a bite, noticing how he wasn't going to reply as I continue, "Where's Kaden?"

"Why?"

There's a moment where a growl threatens to slip past my lips. Instead, I compose myself, stepping closer until there was hardly much space between myself and him. He's stares down at me, expression tense, while I lift my hand to place it firmly against his chest. I can feel his heart under my palm, completely even and unfazed by my presence. He's stronger than I remember. So, I bring my other hand up, putting it on the back of his head to pull him down.

With my lips against his ear, I whisper, "Stop being such a stubborn little-"

I had no time to finish my sentence. He grabbed me tightly, twisting me around until my back was pressed against his front. The sudden movement had me stunned for a good moment.

160

"Oh Dawn, my pretty mate. You know you belong to me, and no one else," he murmurs, his breath drifting down my neck. I try my best not to react too much, but my body betrays me, as my back arches slightly. The touch of my mate is like nothing else.

"Well, isn't this interesting."

Rylan lets me go enough so I stumble forward and glance over my shoulder to see who had interrupted us. Kaden, of all people, Mara, and an unfamiliar man I assume is the bounty hunter from the Discipline pack. They all look at us both with amusement, aside from Mara.

"Kaden, don't make this awkward," she scolds, nudging his side with her elbow.

"Rylan, Dawn, I believe this is the perfect time to introduce you to Tavish; a bounty hunter from the Discipline Pack. He is staying here for a few days while we discuss business," Kaden states.

Tavish is tall and well built, which makes sense, considering his job title. He has ruffled auburn hair and eyes that are a color I've never seen before. It's a mixture of light green and hazel brown. It's not so often discipline pack members leave their pack, so it's different finally meeting one. He stares straight at me, even though it's Rylan who hesitantly walks over to shake his hand.

"Just call me Tav," he says, his tone warm, but his eyes are icy. I stay where I am, not sure if I want to get any closer to him. There's also *no* way I'm about to shake his bare hand.

"What business are you working on? Can I help at all, while I'm here?" Rylan questions.

Kaden shakes his head. "This isn't something we need another opinion on, but thank you, Rylan. Dawn seems to have Millicent's problem covered, that's for sure."

Is he trying to make Rylan mad?

Mara seems to notice, as she nudges Kaden again. When he glances down at her, she frowns, which is an amusing sight to see on her pretty face. It's impressive how well she stands up to Kaden, which can't be an easy feat, and not just because he's the alpha of vengeance.

161

"She does, doesn't she," Rylan says, his voice tight as he turns to look at me. The gaze is only brief, but it chills my blood. "She was just about to take her apple back to her room."

"No I wasn't."

"Dawn ... "

"I was actually hoping to get out for a little while," I say, ignoring the looks of hot fire that I was receiving from Rylan.

He knows I need to get out of this place, even if it's outside for a few moments. Naturally, I would like to shift or something, and truly escape for a few hours, but neither Kaden nor Rylan would let that happen. But perhaps I could convince Rylan to come with me. I would ask Mara, but she has her daughter to look after.

"You've been locked up here for a while, so I'm sure you're desperate to get out," Mara says sympathetically. "I've been working on a garden out back that maybe you could check out if that would help?"

I could have hugged her right there.

"Perhaps Tavish could join you. He's had a long drive here," Kaden adds, and the tension in the room rises beyond belief.

Rylan looks as if he's about to protest, but he's cut off by Tav himself, who steps forward valiantly. He's brave, as I assume he knows Rylan is my mate. Without a mark on my neck, though, I doubt he's afraid to offer anything.

"I would love to do that," he says. "I haven't felt the sun on my back for a few hours now."

I return his smile, trying to come off as polite. Brushing past Rylan, I stand by Tav's side and motion toward the door that leads to the back of the house. I know it's there, since my bedroom is close to the exit. It's been tempting the entire time to escape out that way and get back to the purity pack, where my sister is.

The moment we are alone, I relax. He may be a stranger, but he's not a furious Rylan who wants me locked up in my room. Instead, he's a discipline pack member who hunts people down for a living.

But he's not mad. Thankfully.

"I've heard a lot about you, believe it or not," he says in that thick, drawly accent of the discipline pack.

I give him a sideways look as we walk down the corridor, a little unsure of how to react to that. "From Mara or Kaden?"

"Mara."

That can't be good.

"What did she say about me?" I ask lightly.

This must have something to do with our talk yesterday. The idea of Tav being my other mate is terrifying, especially if I have to deal with an alpha and a bounty hunter. It would be a Fate thing to do though, for his own amusement.

"She mentioned the whole mate thing," he said casually.

My blood ran cold.

He paused, making me stop too. When I turned, he was staring at me, conflict in those strange colored eyes. Then, he held his hand out, and I glanced down at it warily.

"I think we should find out, don't you?"

Chapter Twenty-Eight

Dawn

I stare at his hand, unsure of what I should do.

"Come on," he tempts, pushing his hand out closer to me. I recoil back. No way. He can't be serious right now. Does he understand the consequences if Rylan found out? One of them will die, and with Rylan's temper, I have an idea of who that might be.

I turn on my heel and walk back down the corridor, leaving him where he stood, as I said over my shoulder, "Don't be ridiculous, we aren't mates. I have one."

He knows about what I'm cursed with, but I don't want him to start thinking he truly is my mate. Just because he showed up here out of the blue, doesn't mean Fate decided he would be my mate, even if it does make a lot of sense. But my other mate could be *anyone* in this world, including Tavish, but the likelihood…

The bounty hunter follows me, quickening his steps to match my stride. He doesn't say any more until we find the back door, and I slide it open.

"There is always a possibility. I have wanted a mate for a very long time, so I would like to find out," Tavish says, and I sigh. If it is Tavish, then that means his original mate died a while ago, which is impossible to break to someone. Fate has told me this was like a second chance for them, even if it could ruin Rylan.

Which is why Fate is doing this.

"I was curious, but now I don't want to know who my mate is. Wherever he may be, I think he would be better off without having a mate who he has to share, you included," I tell him, as he joins me outside.

Mara has done a great job making this garden beautiful. It's not completely finished yet, I can tell, with some places just mounds of dirt, but for the most part, she has chosen beautiful flowers and shrubs to decorate the gravel path that lead around it. Tavish doesn't seem to appreciate the selections of roses and snapdragons around the place, which I pause to look at for a few moments, instead of answering his questions.

"For my piece of mind, would you just touch me?" he says in a tame way of begging. I sigh, my fingers brushing off a snow white petal of a rose.

"I don't think my mate would be very pleased to hear you talking to me like that."

I continue down the gravel path. At this point, I'm only wanting to be around him because I want an excuse to be out here without Rylan breathing down my neck. He's furious enough at me. Now, though, I'm starting to wonder whether his company would be less nerve-wracking. At least his touch doesn't have major consequences.

The air is sweet around me as I continue to walk. Tavish isn't making any major moves to touch me, which I'm grateful for. He has respect.

"It is not my fault that this idea was put into my head," Tavish says slowly. I can't agree more. I suppose that's what I get for sharing the information with Mara. "Now it is all I will think about until we can confirm that it is true, or untrue."

I ignore him, continuing down the path. Lucy would love it here.

A few trees curve around us, each in varying size and type. My fingers brush along the bark of the first one. The feeling dances up my fingers, my arms and right to my heart, while I breathe the

165

scent of it into my lungs. No one can disturb that, even Tavish, who strides up behind me.

He proves me wrong.

I was just about to pass the tree by, when he grabbed me, twisting me around until my back was pressed against the tree. All my breath was expelled from body, as Tavish tightly held my shirt sleeves so I had no hope in escape. His unnerving eyes bore into mine, and it suddenly dawned on me how serious he is about this, while I had so easily brushed it off.

"We don't need to resort to this kind of... behavior," I insist slowly, my hands coming up between our chests, ready to push him away with all my strength if it comes to that. I'm hoping it doesn't, but I don't know Tavish. I have no idea what he is really like.

"I just have to know." He breathes. The moment his gaze flickers to my lips, I begin to worry.

My fingers crumple his shirt. "Tavish, let's just talk about this."

"You don't listen-"

"I think you need to step away from my mate."

I glance to my left, where the voice came from. Rylan stood there; his expression darker than I've ever seen it, as he regarded the situation silently. I know angry Rylan. I'm looking at him. For once, it's not focused on me, but the bounty hunter who has me pinned to the tree.

"You know she might be mine," Tavish said gruffly. Wrong move, idiot. He's an alpha. I wish I had time to echo my thoughts into words, but Rylan had already shoved his shoulder back violently.

A flicker of fear expressed itself on Tavish's face for a single second, before he masked it. He could see how prevalent the alpha's anger is, but he wouldn't fear it. His job is to stand up to any danger, even if this is different. Even if Rylan could easily kill him in a single blow. Especially when he's protecting his mate.

"Rylan," I hear someone say from the foot of the garden. It was Kaden, rushing out to see the commotion that was just about to

166

unfold in front of us. Mara is beside him, concern written across her face.

"It's just a little misunderstanding," Tavish says arrogantly.

Rylan is about to beat that smile off his face, I can tell, even if his back is to me. I don't blame him. A part of me wants him to, but I decide against it, as Rylan shoves Tavish back again. He loses his balance, stumbling backward a few more steps.

"No one ... " Rylan growled, "touches Dawn."

"That's enough," Kaden snapped, grabbing the back of Tavish's shirt to pull him out of the way so that he was in front of Rylan.

Clearly blind with anger, Rylan swung back and hit Kaden straight in the face.

It was a good hit. The force was undeniably strong, as it completely turned Kaden's head to the side, blood immediately erupting from his nose. His muscles tensed, but he didn't fight back. He probably thought what is point? When Rylan gets like this, he's unstoppable. He could probably take down an immortal in a fight.

"This has to stop," I insist, grabbing Rylan's arm to turn him to face me. The sparks are enough to knock some sense into him. An ounce of his anger dies down a little when he looks at me.

Out of the corner of my eyes, I see Kaden stumble toward Mara, who grabs his face to inspect the damage done. Tavish is nowhere to be seen.

"You're okay." I breathe, pulling Rylan closer to embrace him. "I'm okay."

He's tense. My heart squeezes with guilt; I should have never messed with him like this. As much as he doesn't want to admit it, he's fragile like this, the veil of coping having been slowly stripped with the year I spent away from him. He still trembles against me, trying to calm down the anger I hate so much.

"We can talk about this later. Right now, I'm going to take you back to your room," I whisper in his ear, and he nods.

As infuriated as I am with Rylan, still, for the lying and the faking, I care for him. This anger and pain that he feels is all my fault, and he doesn't deserve it.

***

Rylan didn't come with me to dinner.

I made sure he stayed in his room, since Tavish would be joining us. He's sleeping now, I hope. It didn't take as much convincing as I thought it would. Just a simple kiss on the cheek and a promise I would join him in bed afterwards. To sleep. Strictly.

Little was said at dinner. Kaden sported a black eye, and Mara kept sending wary glances his way as if she was worried about his well-being.

But no one mentions what happened.

Tavish sat right next to me as we ate, which was not at all my intention. Luckily, we were distracted as someone new decided to join us for dinner. Kace, Kaden's brother, who nearly killed me by hanging me straight out the window. The look I gave him as he walked in was hostile, but I made no move to cause any more drama.

Kaden and Kace began talking about things completely beyond me. I took that time to truly examine Kace.

I will have to remember to ask him where those scars on his face had come from. Other than that, he had a rather flawless complexion, with those dark eyes and hair. He is one of those people who conceal their emotions brilliantly.

All of a sudden I feel a hand on my thigh, my bare thigh.

I immediately shoot my gaze over to Tavish. I know it's him. That doesn't surprise me. What does, is the feeling that comes from his touch.

Or lack thereof.

Nothing. No sparks. We aren't mates. All this has been for nothing. Kaden took a hit for him, and we aren't even mates.

I let out an exhale of relief.

Kace got up to use the restroom at the same time Mara noticed the expression on my face. Pure elation. I can't wait to go back and tell Rylan he has nothing to worry about, that my mate isn't here.

"Everything okay?" Mara asks lightly, tilting her head with curiosity.

"Everything is brilliant," I reply. When I look at Tavish, I can't decipher his expression. He looks lost. I assume he built up the idea, and had to fully believe that we were mates. Now that it has been revealed that we aren't, he doesn't know what to do.

By the time Kace has come back, I'm finished. He offers to clean up everyone's plates, so the staff don't have to do it.

It was that split decision that had to be up to Fate. He would have manipulated it to happen.

Because, as he leaned over me to grab my plate, his bare hand brushed me, right on my knuckles. We both jerk back, Kace dropping the plate so it shatters on the ground. I think my heart did the exact same thing.

Sparks. Kace is my other mate.

Chapter Twenty-Nine

Dawn

If Fate was standing in front of me right now, I probably would have strangled him.

There is no way. *No way.* Kace tried to kill me, and even if it was all a part of Rylan's sick plan, it still mattered to me. Fate has *really* outdone himself with this one, and not only has it left me speechless, but also I feel stupid. Of course he would pair me with Kace.

Just to rile Rylan up.

Kace looks mortified. It was close to the look on his face when he was caught trying to shove me out the window by Rylan. This look expresses so much shock, that I was convinced for a moment that maybe he would pass out.

I think I might do the same thing, as I slide my chair back, the scrape of it against the floor drowning within the pounding of my ears. I can feel the rest of the room staring at Kace and me from my side vision, but my gaze is completely locked in his. This can't be happening. I don't *want* this to happen.

The back of my mind decided to pipe up. This is for Rylan's pack... My pack. This is for Kaden, and Mara, and everyone.

But I felt a part of me fall away.

"This can't be real," Kace whispers, his voice trembling as much as his entire body is. At this point, he has backed away from me, having no idea of the deal that transpired between Fate and I. "This can't... you already have a mate."

"What's going on?" Kaden questions, although I have a feeling he has an idea of what just passed between us.

Kace has gone completely pale as he continues to stare at me like I'm crazy. He holds the wrist of the hand that touched me, moving his gaze between that, and me. My heart aches at the sight of it. Kace's real mate died years ago, so when I choose Rylan to mark me at the end of this, he will have no one.

Kace drags his wary gaze over to Kaden. "She's my mate."

The look on Karen's face is confused for a moment, as he clearly struggles to understand what he is hearing. This is his brother, who would take over as alpha if he and Mara passed.

"I have to tell Rylan," I say softly, the weight of my own words settling on my shoulders. Perhaps he could handle Tavish, but this? Kace seems to come to that realization also, as he backs away, and leaves the room without looking back, the door banging against the wall in his wake.

***

I knock on Rylan's door softly.

"Come in," a muffled reply comes through, and I slowly push the door open. Rylan lays in bed, shirtless, sheets pulled up to the bottom of his ribs. He looks a little lost, as he lies there, head turned to me. My heart practically falls into my stomach.

Slowly, I close the door behind me, and come to sit down on the edge of his bed. Rylan sits up, silent, clearly expecting the worst.

"Tavish isn't my mate," I tell him softly, peaking my gaze up enough to watch his expression; relief, then a slight hint of anger. It's hard to take him seriously when he hasn't got a shirt on and his hair is all mussed and scattered like that. Maybe he did get sleep. I hope so; that way he won't be so mad when he hears the truth about my other mate.

171

"That's good," he murmurs. "I don't understand why you touched him, though."

I slide closer to him, sensing the tension he is feeling. Perhaps that is a perk of being his mate. I can tell exactly when he is on the edge. "He touched me, actually."

Rylan inhales slowly, before he pulls the covers back, motioning for me to come slide in beside him. I kick my shoes off before I do so. I may be wearing a dress, but it still feels delightful to sidle in next to him like that, his familiar scent consuming me. As soon as I lie down, he wraps his arm around my shoulder, pulling me close.

For a moment, I didn't want to tell him about Kace. All I want to do is lay with my head on his chest, and for once, admire my time with my mate. But I can't do that. Rylan deserves the truth, no matter how much it might destroy the both of us.

"I did, however, find out who my other mate is," I say softly, running my hand down his chest to his stomach. He tenses under me.

"What did you say?"

He suddenly leans over me, his hands by my shoulder, his lower body pinning mine to the bed. His silvery blue eyes blaze not only with curiosity, but confusion. He looks terrified and slight betrayed. I reach my hand up to brush his face gently, hoping my touch will be able soothe the anger I know will soon brew under the surface.

"Kace," I say, slightly cringing as I await his reaction. "It was an accident, but we touched, and the spark was definitely there."

Rylan's left eye twitches, then his jaw ticks. It's the silent anger that scares me the most, but I keep my hand on his face, my thumb rhythmically rubbing the line of his jaw while I watch him. He swallows, before he closes his eyes. He definitely believes me. I don't know why he wouldn't. He believes that all of a sudden, he's sharing me with another male, one who is one of the most unpredictable that we know.

"Did it feel like ours?" he asks, voice slightly shaking at the edges. I have to actually consider that for a moment.

172

"Not quite," I relay, sifting through my memories. This isn't a lie either. When I first touched Rylan, I associated the feeling at first with the end of my free life. Then, later, when I started to get sick and crave his touch, I associated it with the greatest pleasure in the world. More than an alpha like Asher could have given me.

With Kace, I felt nothing like that.

"It was more distant. When I think it through, it's clearly been fabricated by a change in timeline. Fate has done his job, but the feeling is nowhere near as *real* and as *addictive* as yours is," I tell him honestly.

He considered my expression for a moment, searching for any sign of a lie. When he doesn't see one, I see him visibly relax a little more.

"You can reject him," he says, tilting his head slightly.

I frown at him. "He might not survive that."

Rylan doesn't care. For all he cares, Kace could die from the rejection of his mate, and Rylan would continue on with his life with me with no complications or interruptions. The extent of Rylan's anger and potential devilish activities are unknown to me, so I'm not sure whether or not I can fully trust him with this.

"Plus," I decide to add, "it might change something with Fate's deal, and we don't want to have gone through all this just for it to end with nothing."

Rylan still didn't look convinced. Then something changed.

His entire body tensed again, and the Rylan I knew was gone. It was almost as if all his body heat had disappeared. His eyes darkened to unfamiliarity. I went to say something, but I couldn't. I'm not scared of Rylan, but this isn't Rylan. The moment I try to push away from him, he grabs my wrist and stops me.

"What are you-"

Before I can do or say any more, Rylan lets go of my wrist to press it against my neck. How he knew that would bring unconsciousness, I don't have time to question, before it swallows me whole.

173

I rolled my neck back, hearing something protest.

A lot of me aches. My back, my neck and even my butt. When I open my eyes, I realize I'm sitting on concrete, which explains it. A wall behind me has been keeping my body propped up, and by the painful feeling that plagues the entirety of my body, I've been left here for a while.

A door on the other side of the room opens. In response, I clamber to my feet, ignoring the protest of my limbs while I keep my back pressed right against the wall.

The man walking through the door is Rylan. Of course it is. Right now, all I want to do is kill him, to strangle him until he tells me why he would betray me like this.

I should have never trusted him…

"I hate you," I murmur as he walks closer. He's so casual, hands shoved in his pockets as he strolls toward me, pausing in front of me. I make a silent vow in my head to never move from my place against the wall.

"Finally, you're awake," he mutters sardonically.

"I'll never trust you again," I growl under my breath.

He sighs deeply. I can hardly recognize him. The man I'm staring at isn't my mate, but a complete stranger. Those eyes I began to love so much aren't just sallow and dark, but almost dead, as if the light has been sucked out of them.

I look around, seeing nothing familiar about this room at all. That's what the terrifying part is.

"Rylan isn't here anymore, Dawn," he says menacingly. "Right now, you're talking to Sinful."

Chapter Thirty

Dawn

I take a moment to absorb the information.

Sinful.

The only hint that Rylan is gone is his eyes. The depth of the raw emotion is too unfamiliar to grasp. Like two onyx stones, his eyes are on me, his gaze unrelenting. I've seen that smile before. That's the scary part.

"Why?" I breathe, shifting to my feet so I could have some leverage with him. "Why are you doing this?"

I don't know anything about Sinful, but already I hate him. I had no idea one could possess the power to completely take over someone's body like that, so seeing it happen right in front of me is terrifying. There is a brewing anger within me that urges me to launch myself at him, but I've been witness to Rylan's strength. If Sinful can harness that ...

"You're not going to ask what happened to your precious mate?" he questions, seeming genuinely surprised. He even sounds *exactly* like Rylan, which sends a shiver down my spine. This is definitely Sinful though ... a part of me can just feel it.

"What did you do to him?" I growl.

I'm not sure how I would react if he told me Rylan was dead. I may not be marked, but it would hurt, and I surely don't want to pursue a relationship with Kace, even if he *is* my other mate.

Maybe I would end up dying ... No, Dawn a month ago would never even consider that as an option. Especially because of Lucy.

"He's fine, don't worry. He's trapped somewhere in the back of this mind until I'm done with you," Sinful tells me, and a tremor consumes my body.

I don't say another thing. There's no point. Sinful is the only one here who is going to explain what is going to happen, and I can't do anything but listen.

"As for why, well, I'm here to talk to you about the deal you made with Fate."

I freeze. "Which one?"

"I believe you agreed to have the moon goddess admit her love to her mate. Can I ask why that hasn't happened yet?" he questions, folding his arms across his chest. I watch the movement, angered by it. How can he completely take over Rylan's body with no hint of remorse? Especially to bring this up...

"I've been too busy dealing with this other mate of mine," I snap. "I didn't think you had any idea of Fate's deal with me, anyway."

Fate had gone along with it because Sinful didn't know. At least that's what I thought...

"Of course I knew," he says with a raised eyebrow. He tells me this as if I have any idea of the extent of his power. In reality, I know hardly anything about him, other than what I have been told. He's the Devil. I can see it. "Now, I would like to give you the option to see your mate again, if you agree to do this."

At this point, I'm curious.

If Sinful is so interested in Millicent, the moon goddess, then I want to know why. "You took over the alpha of purity's body just to tell me *this?*"

There is a moment where I'm convinced he looks wary of answering my question. Rylan can keep his emotions pretty well hidden when he wants to, so it takes a split second for him to mask

176

it. Especially in his eyes. Those deep, soulless eyes whose persona behind it is something I don't want to get to know.

"Perhaps you'll see if you do finally make her agree," Sinful says testily, and I fold my arms, matching his current stance. "*When* you make her agree."

"What do I get out of it?" I ask.

A faint smile graces his features. "You had a deal, remember? The goddess will get her precious powers back, and you can all be happy. Also, your mate back of course. Your first one …"

Hearing him say it like that has me clenching my jaw to keep my mouth shut. Kace's original mate died long ago, which gave Fate and Sinful the perfect opportunity to use him as their puppet. For that alone, I want to hurt them, but I refuse to give Sinful the pleasure. He already has Rylan's life on the line.

"Fine," I snap. "But she is the one who makes the decision in the end, so don't find yourself blaming that on me."

"Fair enough. Although, I warn you, this *must* happen," he informs me sternly.

I don't mention the fact that I haven't even met Millicent yet, which is going to make this even more difficult achieve. He might already know that, if he is as powerful as I'm lead to believe he is.

"Can I have Rylan back now?" I ask softly. There is nothing else I want right now than to see my mate's blue eyes again, and to feel his arms around me once again.

Sinful seems to think for a moment. "Maybe tomorrow."

My eyes widen, as he starts to back away. No, *no*. My steps match his, as I refuse to believe that he is going to keep me from my mate for another day, when I don't even have an idea of where he has taken me.

"Please, Sinful … I need to see him," I beg, although it's probably falling on deaf ears. Why would the devil want anything good for me?

"You have the rest of your life to be with Rylan, until he dies of old age and you live on as a phantom wolf. Maybe you'll need

177

Kace?" he says, much to my disgust. Is Kace a phantom wolf too? "And anyways, I want to see your reaction when you realize I'm going to leave every door in this place open for you to escape, if you choose."

***

This is a moral dilemma.

Can I trust Rylan to find me again? Do I want him to find me? Of course I do... but if I step through this door, I'll be lost somewhere unknown, if my assumptions are correct. Plus, I'll be leaving Rylan here, if Sinful is true to his word.

If I stay, though, I'm done for. If I get roped into another one of his deals, I doubt I'll be able to find out. I've weighed up why Sinful wants to let me go, and I've decided it's because he wants to see if I'll leave Rylan here. But he's an alpha... he could find me again. I know it.

At least I hope I do. He wouldn't want to stay here, though.

I push the door open, and I'm shocked at what I see. I assumed this door would lead out to somewhere horrible owned by the cruelest soul to exist. Instead, I'm in an unfamiliar room. A bedroom.

The door closed behind me. There is something about this room that does have a hint of familiarity tied to it. The way room is dressed is similar to my one back in the vengeance pack.

Did Sinful send me straight back again?

I turn to open the door, wanting to get straight back in to get Rylan back. Instead, it's a hallway, with someone walking down it. Quickly, I close the door, looking back into the room. Whoever it belongs to, they have rather dark tastes, considering the black carpet and duvet set. I wish there was some hint as to who the room belongs to, but there is nothing from first glance.

The door opens slowly, and someone walks in. It's Kace.

We stare at each other, both completely bewildered by the current situation. Of all the places Sinful could have sent me, I've walked straight into the room of my other mate. I wish the door led me straight off the edge of any cliff, anywhere.

"Dawn," Kace says warily, "what are you doing in my room?"

I'm completely lost for words for various reasons. He looks ... unbelievable. Before he was my mate, I saw nothing but a terrible man who wanted me dead. Now, he looks almost perfect, like how I see Rylan.

I shake my head. "I was kidnapped."

"Kidnapped?" he questions in disbelief, stepping forward to grab hold of both my arms. I ignore the feeling that it brings. "How ... when?"

"Sinful took me. He got into Rylan's body, or something, and now Rylan is who knows where, and I left him behind," he tell him quickly, feeling each and every emotion piling on after each other, weighing down on my shoulders. I want to cry, to scream... I hate myself for leaving him there, even if Sinful promised to give him back.

Kace leads me over to sit on the edge of his bed before my legs give out on me.

"It's okay," Kace murmurs, his arm coming around me. "Kaden will do anything to get him back, and I can tell you he is brilliant at finding people."

"Then let's go tell him right now," I insist, but Kace catches my arm before I can stand.

"Not now, you're hurt."

I shake my head at him. Hurt? I don't have time to be hurt right now, and I hardly feel the pain. That is, until Kace touches my forehead, and I cringe. Then his dark gaze flutters down to my neck, which his fingertips softly brush over.

"What did he do to you?" he asks gently. I swallow, before I'm on my feet. I refuse to think about myself until Rylan is here. Safe.

Kace jumps up as well. "We will find him, I promise. You stay here until I get Kaden. You need to rest."

Completely broken and feeling utterly useless, I grit my teeth and fall back to sit on the bed. He is right. I won't be able to find Rylan, but Kaden surely will.

I watch Kace leave the room before I lie back to pray for the first time, that someone out there, might be able to bring him back to me.

Chapter Thirty-One

Dawn

The moment I could no longer hear Kace's footsteps, I was on my feet.

It's not Kace's fault at all. It's mine. I need to get back to my room, because at least there, I can't smell his scent, or even accidently fall asleep in his bed. So, I'll go back, shower, and start plotting a way to get Rylan back.

No one sees me on my way back. Once I'm at my room, I make sure my door is closed, before I take some clothes from the drawer, and take them to the shower. I feel so guilty for everything that has happened. My feet drags, as if shackles were locked around my ankles. What if this was Fate's idea? If I never get Rylan back, then I will be forced by nature to be with Kace. I don't think I could live with that decision.

I shower everything off me. Washing my hair, my face, my entire body, I try rid myself of any ounce of Sinful on my body, wishing my troubles would go down the drain with it.

Who even is Sinful? What does he look like when he isn't stealing other people's bodies?

Once I'm out of the shower, I try myself change and dress. My entire body is numb, while my mind races. I hadn't expected to walk through that door to make it back here. That means Rylan could be anywhere in the pack quarter, or out of it, for that matter. Who knows where Sinful resides?

181

Once I had done drying my hair, I put my towel down and walked out of the bathroom, only to see him standing there.

Rylan.

He looks awfully ... normal. His eyes are back, that silvery blue moonlight slightly dulled down, but they were back. He was back, I think.

We stand there staring at each other. Rylan is by the front door, as if he had just walked in. He is dressed the way he was when Sinful had taken him over, his clothes now slightly rumpled, as if he has struggled at some point. His skin is sallow, and he looks paler than usual. That doesn't bother me, though.

I take a few steps toward him, wondering if he is real, or if I've gone so crazy, I'm hallucinating. He only watches me silently, waiting for me to make the first move.

My feet only stop when I am right in front of him. He looks down at me, looking regretful, as if he is reflecting my own expression. I raise my hand slowly, bringing it forward to place it on his chest. He's gloriously warm, and under my palm, I can feel the faint beat of his heart. Rylan keeps quiet, watching my movements carefully.

Without having any real control over my body, I move my hand, instead wrapping my arms around him, pulling myself close enough until my head takes the place of where my hand had been.

"Is this really you?" I ask breathlessly.

His arms come around me, smoothly rubbing down my back in a way of comfort. I lean further into the touch, letting the relief of his presence wash over me. For a while there, I was convinced I would never see Rylan again. I don't know the extent of Sinful's power, so seeing him here in front of me is shocking, but I'm not about to complain.

"Of course," he murmurs into my hair, not ceasing the stroking of my back. "He's gone now."

"Thank the goddess," I mutter, pulling away slightly to look up at him. Other than the clear emotional distress that he has been through, which is written across his face, he doesn't looked harmed in any other way.

I pull away slightly. "How did you get away?"

"He let me go," Rylan replies, much to my surprise. What is Sinful's game? He must be incredibly infatuated with having Millicent admit her love for her mate for him to use Rylan against me, and then let him go right after.

"Well, I guess I have to talk to the moon goddess," I say airily, his threat loitering in the back of my mind. I'm afraid that at any second now, he will take Rylan again.

The last thing I thought I would see on Rylan's face right now just appeared. A smile. A playful one too.

He pulls at my arm, dragging me over to my bed. It's been unmade, since I believed I would be spending the night in Rylan's bed last night. I fall back onto the feather duvet, sinking into the softness of it. Rylan only watches me fall, standing above me for a few moments, only watching. I'm pleased he is being assertive, but I'm also a little worried about what he has planned.

"Shouldn't you be resting after all that?" I question coyly, tilting my head best I can on the bed. "Not pushing your mate onto the bed when the ceremony is still a few weeks away."

"I always have energy for you," he reminds me, to which I reply with a roll of my eyes.

He leans over me in a way that has my heart racing. Only Rylan could make me feel this way. I open my arms to beckon him closer to me. He smiles, his dark hair falling over his eyes as he leans even closer, letting me place my hands on the hard planes of his back, the thin cotton of his shirt is the only barrier from feeling the sparks.

I'm not going to mention Kace. I don't even want to think about him.

"It hasn't been long, but I hardly remember the hate I felt for you," I admit to him. Sometimes I forget why I did, when I'm around him, and I'm able to feel the full extent of the mate bond.

183

"You had every right to hate me. You need freedom, and I thought I could change you," he tells me. "If it wasn't for the mate bond, you would still hate me, but I think you have a little more trust for me now. You understand that I want the best for you at all times, and a part of you has accepted that."

Moving my hand, I cup his face softly. "I think you're right."

Rylan smiled, bringing his face down to kiss me. He stopped though, pausing right before his lips touched mine. I frowned, waiting for him to disclose his hesitation.

"What if Sinful still has control over me?" he asks distractedly.

He pulls away so his arms are extended beside my head. The look on his face is of pure distress, as if he has convinced himself that Sinful still has a hold on his body. I'm not sure how he would know that, but a part of me knows this isn't Sinful. Sinful wouldn't say that long speech that is completely true. Sinful doesn't know me like Rylan does.

"I doubt that," I reassure him, brushing the hair back from his forehead. It only falls back down again. "Your eyes aren't black. And as your mate, I know it's really you, not Sinful."

Rylan still doesn't look very convinced.

"Ask me something that only I would know... something from our past that I should have remembered, that Sinful couldn't lie about," he insists. I know for a fact that he isn't Sinful. That devil had no problem admitting to me who he was, and didn't allow Rylan any control over his body.

I decide to give Rylan a little confirmation, as I scrape through my mind for something he should know. I have an idea, although it hurts a little to bring it up again. I decide to do it anyway, hoping he remembered this night as well as I have.

"What did I say to you when I agreed to meet you in the square? What my last words before your guards knocked me unconscious?" I question, trying not to wince as I remember how harshly I said it. Back then, I'd meant those words too, with every fiber of my body, I really did, back then.

"You said you hated me." He breathes hoarsely. "I don't think I will ever forget that night for the rest of my life."

I pull Rylan back down to kiss me, my impatience not letting me wait another second. There is a big part of me that wants to wipe away that exact memory from his mind. In fact, I would like to wipe every sour memory he has of me now.

Rylan responds instantly, the kiss slow and gentle, as he refuses to let me heat it up, no matter how insistent I'm being. I don't press it though, after seeing directly what he went through.

He pulls away, much to my surprise, leaving me breathless as he looks down at me. "I have something I need to show you."

I narrow my eyes at him, as he pushes himself off the bed, walking to the door. I'm stunned, as he opens it, looking over his shoulder expectantly, willing me to follow. I get up, deciding to follow him, since he's ignoring my questions and protests.

"Rylan ... you've just had your mind violated, and you're wanting to do this? You just got back," I exclaim, following him down the corridor.

I hear him chuckle. "I have something to show you, that I'm sure you will like."

Chapter Thirty-Two

Dawn

"How did you orchestrate this?" I question, not yet knowing what I'm about to see, as I walk down the hallway with Rylan at my side.

He seems genuinely excited for this. "I planned it before any of this happened. It just happened to arrive today."

I give him a sideways look, wondering what he's insinuating. Shaking my head in disbelief, I don't say another word, instead just following his instructions on where to go. I don't get another hint out of him as we walk into the foyer, Rylan's hand comes to rest on the small of my back, as if to stop me wanting to turn around and run back in the other direction.

However, the moment I see the special surprise, I know I'm not going anywhere.

Lucy. He brought Lucy back to me.

She almost looks different, even though it's hardly been two weeks since I've last seen her. Ultimately, she is still her beautiful self, with a little more on her height, and on the ends of her hair. She's healthy, though, which is the most important thing.

Her face breaks into a brilliant smile that I'm sure matches mine. I throw my arms around her, wishing I could hug every inch of her to check if she's actually real.

"I missed you so much," she whispered in my ear. I let her go, holding her shoulders so I can properly examine her.

"How did you look after yourself?" I question in disbelief. "You look great!"

Lucy was probably relieved to have some time without me. She's one of the most independent people I know, and has managed to grow up trying to look after herself, and clearly nothing has changed. I'm still angry at Rylan for taking me here without her, but it's a relief to have her back again.

"Rylan had a few people there to keep an eye on me," she tells me, more to quell my own worries rather than answer the question honestly. "And yes, I have had everything explained to me."

I glance over my shoulder at Rylan, who watches me carefully. I think the smile on my face is answer enough that I'm grateful for what he has done. He knows I love my sister, so the fact that he has brought her back to me has me beaming with happiness. It's as if in that moment my other mate doesn't exist.

Footsteps from the other side of the room catch my attention, and when I look over, it's Kaden, holding a small child in his arms.

For a moment, he looks startled at the sight of Rylan as he walks closer. "I heard news that you were taken."

As Rylan answers Kaden, I focus more on the girl in his arms. She is younger than five, I assume, and clearly is Kaden and Mara's child. She has Mara's brilliant golden hair that has been pulled back in an attempt at a ponytail insinuating that it was Kaden's doing. Her eyes are like the alpha's though. They are dark, near to black, as she stares at me. And just like her father's eyes, they are cold and raise the hairs on my arms.

"Who's this?" Lucy asks softly, referring to the young girl in Kaden's arms. Lucy has always loved kids, so it doesn't surprise me that she is reaching out for attention from the little girl, who if I remember correctly, is named Shaye.

Kaden seems pleased that his daughter is drawing him out of conversation with Rylan. These two still seem uneasy around each other.

"This is Shaye," Kaden says, confirming my original thought. "She can speak, she's just a little shy, like her mother."

187

Lucy smiles at Shaye, but the young girl turns her gaze away, shoving her face back into the front of Kaden's shirt. If we are staying here longer, then I'm sure Lucy will sway the girl into falling in love with her like everyone else who meets her does. Even the most shy of people end up opening themselves up to her.

I notice Kaden staring at me now. "You might want to talk to Kace, he's really stressing out about this."

I can almost feel Rylan tensing up.

"Kace?" I hear Lucy say. She mustn't have had *everything* explained to her just yet. This might be too much to explain to her right now, since she just arrived, and I just got Rylan back from Sinful.

"Why don't we go have dinner together, get everything back on normal terms again?" Kaden offers, cutting the conversation away from Kace. "I think Mara was getting something together with some of her helpers. She would love to meet you Lucy, I'm sure."

That lightened the mood a little. At least with Lucy. Rylan clearly doesn't want to be going to dinner with Kace there, but at the same time, the last time I went alone, that was how I found out we were mates in the first place. He wouldn't listen if I told him to stay up in his room.

I don't want him to do anything to Kace, or the other way around.

There are no more words spoken as Kaden leads us to the dining room. Lucy holds my hand while she looks at Shaye, who hangs over the alpha of vengeance's shoulder.

No one is in the dining room when we get there. I'm more grateful that Kace isn't there, if I'm honest. I sit beside Rylan, expecting Lucy to then take my other side, however, she goes to sit next to Shaye. I know instantly that she has lost interest in me and the story of Kace, as she is now concentrating on the little girl who still seems uneasy around her.

"You promise you won't act out with Kace tonight?" I question lowly to Rylan, so Lucy wouldn't catch it. The last thing I want to do is have her thinking there are more problems with our relationship.

Even though there are. Very evidently.

Rylan's expression is stony cold and indifferent, but his eyes are wary, as he replies, "I'll try my best."

Kace comes in around ten minutes later. At that point, Rylan was busy discussing what happened with Sinful, while I listen half-heartedly, concentrating more on what Lucy and Shaye were getting up to. My sister has taken it upon herself to help her eat her dinner while Kaden was on the other side, watching for anything wrong.

He looked over the table, assessing the situation. Conversation ceased as my gaze turned to Kace, who went to sit beside Kaden, right in front of me. He doesn't even acknowledge Rylan, as if he wasn't surprised he was back after I had freaked out earlier.

"Are you okay?" Kace asks me softly, raising an eyebrow at me. It's his way of addressing the Rylan situation without having to talk, or even look at the alpha.

"She's fine," Rylan cuts in before I could talk.

I frown, nudging him under the table. Already, I can tell this isn't going to be an easy dinner to get through. Mara, who had come out with dinner not long before Kace showed up, decides to start another conversation. Both Kace and Rylan seem reluctant to add themselves to that situation, but with another nudge from me to Rylan, and a kick under the table at Kace, they join in.

While we eat, I'm tense, and beside me, Rylan is too. He keeps glancing over at Kace, as if the man would lash out at any second.

I've decided there can't be anything worse in the world than having two mates.

"So, Rylan," Kace says suddenly, when Mara has paused her conversation. "How could you let Sinful take you over like that, and put our mate in danger? I thought alphas were supposed to be strong...."

Oh no.

189

Rylan's fork clatters loudly on his plate, making me cringe. "You shouldn't be calling her your mate. Once I have mated her, the bond will be broken, and you will be left without a mate."

I'm taken aback by the cold edge to Rylan's voice. This is the Rylan who I saw brief flickers of back in the purity pack. The Rylan he had been keeping from me earlier and hiding away. Still, we haven't spoken about it, even though it makes me curious to know where it comes from.

"You never answered my question, Alpha," Kace says, an arrogant air about him, letting Rylan know that he isn't affected... especially with the way he is referring to him as alpha.

It's as if he knows how to wind him up. Just like I did some time ago.

"There's little point in that," Rylan replies slowly, in a patronizing manner. "You clearly don't have the intellect to understand, considering your lack of knowledge about Sinful as it is."

"Well, you must understand that at this time, Dawn is my mate, and you putting her in danger like this is not appreciated. Perhaps you're not in the right state of mind to be around her so often, if you're so susceptible to having your mind taken over by this Sinful man you speak of."

Rylan's jaw visibly clenched, his hands tightening on the edge of the table. It is Kaden who speaks up before me.

"You should shut your mouth, brother. Rylan has taken down a strong man before for touching Dawn, so I would tread lightly. Maybe he could even take me down, if it came down to it," Kaden reminds his brother, who doesn't look so convinced.

I shoot Kaden a grateful look. "He's right. There's no point in fighting."

"I'm perfectly capable of being around my mate," Rylan continues, completely passing off our words of warning. I place my hand on his arm, but he seems unfazed by that as well. "And nothing you can say is going to change that."

190

"It was me who was there for Dawn when you were still dealing with your little Sinful problem," Kace replies, and I cringe.

"You guys need to stop. Not now, in front of Shaye-"

Before I even had a chance to finish my sentence, Lucy attacked. Her hand wrapped around her fork, and in a flurry of movement, she launched over the child and Kaden to attack Kace.

Kaden's reaction was faster than anyone's. He grabbed Lucy, pulling her backwards away from Kace.

His face had clearly been cut, right beside his eye. Had she been a seat closer, his eye would be gone. I can only take my gaze away from Kace, and the blood now streaming down the side of his face, to my sister.

She looks furious, not at all affected by what she has done. She looks at me; her eyes feral.

"He needs to die," she whispers.

Chapter Thirty-Three

Dawn

Lucy looked practically unrecognizable.

There's a wild look in her eyes, as she silently slides back into her chair, right after Kaden had let her go. She trembles under everyone's scrutiny, looking as if she had been shocked into utter silence. I am too. That wasn't my sister who attacked Kace ... my mind goes to Sinful, but I brush it off.

Sinful has to be done with me. I haven't had a chance to speak with Millicent just yet. At this point, I would rather perhaps Rylan or Kaden talk to her instead.

She's the goddess. It's not necessarily an easy conversation to have.

Kace looks at me for help, as he says, "I don't understand...."

I want to tell him neither do I, because that's the truth. But right now, I'm ignoring my other mate as he holds the side of his face that bleeds profusely. I focus on my sister. Right now, I know her well enough to know she's not about to speak. She has that drawn off look about her that usually only appears when she's shy, when I'm the one who has to speak for her.

"Her life has changed so much in the past few weeks," I say uneasily, feeling Rylan's gaze on the side of my face. "She's just not used to you all yet, and she's grown up fearing the alpha of vengeance."

"Of course, we understand," Rylan says, shooting a gaze at Kace. "Right?"

He grits his teeth, but nods. He has to, it's his mate's sister. Lucy, however, doesn't look convinced by the excuse I've created for her. Instead of staying around to hear the rest of the conversation, she's up on her feet, and running out the room, leaving us all at the table in shocked silence.

"Seriously, she tried to kill me," Kace says softly, completely aghast. He doesn't have to hold his emotions back anymore.

"Don't be ridiculous," I snap, "she's not even a teenager."

Kaden hasn't said anything yet. He simply sits there, brooding, while Mara busies herself with feeding Shaye. I should go after Lucy, but there's no use. The poor girl will shut herself up for a while, not wanting to talk to a single person until she's calmed down and reasonable.

Kace gets up and leaves. I don't blame him; Lucy did quite a number on him, even though she is young. That girl has lived in the wild for years, so I don't doubt she could put up a fight against him.

I won't tell him that though.

I feel Rylan's hand on my shoulder. "We should go back up to the room. Lucy should be fine by tomorrow."

He's right. Solemnly, I follow Rylan back up to the room. The moment we step into the room, I close the door behind us, lean against it, and sink to the ground. I mutter, "I'm a terrible sister."

Rylan frowns. He crouches down in front of me, leaning his arm out to brush a hair out of my face. There's sympathy there, for both me and Lucy. At this exact moment, I hate Kace for ever trying to question Rylan's love for me, or how well he can look after me. When I look in his eyes, I can't imagine anyone else being able to understand me better now.

"You're not a terrible sister. Don't think about it for tonight. I saw all over your face that you know it's a useless feat to pursue," Rylan reassures me, and I sigh. He may be right, but it doesn't make me feel any less terrible about myself.

Slowly, I get to my feet, before I clamber into bed. Rylan follows after me, pulling his shirt off while I just fall with defeat.

I feel his hand on my back, while I have my face shoved in the pillow.

"You should probably get changed," Rylan advises tentatively, clearly trying not to push me over the edge of my emotions. I feel him tug affectionately on the back of my shirt; his attempts at promoting me to change not going unnoticed.

I rolled over as he pulled his pants down. He usually sleeps with only his underwear on, which I have accepted. Sometimes the feeling of the sparks between us help me sleep if I wake up from a nightmare. Although, I do prefer to dress up more than him in bed. If I fall asleep in these clothes right now, it won't make much of a difference to most other nights.

"I just want to sleep," I grumble, my voice muffled by the pillow.

Rylan chuckles, as he slides under the bedsheets. On my side, I haven't attempted that much. I'm afraid that if I move, I'll go running to Lucy and make things worse. As if Ryan can read my thoughts, his arms come around me, pressing me securely against his front.

"You're right, she's had it hard, and a lot of that is my fault," Rylan says against my hair. I glare up at him. No way is he trying to put some of this blame on him.

"I don't know," I say uneasily. "She's never been like that."

Rylan sighs. "Tomorrow."

He leans over to switch the light off, while I continue to lay with my clothes completely on. It feels uncomfortable, but I'm not shedding all my clothes off with Rylan right beside me. When I lay my head on his chest though, an answered question comes into my mind. I'm not sure why, but a part of me is curious, and I doubt I'll be able to sleep until I ask. And anyway, it has taken my thoughts away from the subject of Lucy.

"Remember when you told me you had been with other girls in... you know, that way," I start. I feel him tense. "Can I know who, since you know about Asher?"

His exhale is slow and calculated, as he considers how to answer this question. I know I won't have any idea of who the girls are that he might mention; I'm more curious to know about how the circumstances came along. He managed to convince me that he was an innocent angel, which only has me more curious about the girls who agreed to it.

Well, I can think of a lot. The kind of girls who sleep with an alpha to brag about it.

"There was only one girl. It's a long story I don't really want to tell my mate," he says uneasily. I sit up a little more, letting him know he isn't about to get out of this one without an explanation. He sighs, even though he can't see the expression on my face.

"You know about Asher...."

"Yes, but I don't know if there were anymore," he points out, and I growl lowly in response. Is this him assuming, or genuinely wondering?

"There weren't," I say, then reconsider, "there were two, but I was an idiot when I was a teenager, trust me. Now, stop evading the question and tell me about this girl who wasn't your mate."

I'm surprised he didn't mention anything about Kace, after my jab at him about another mate. Instead, he continues on with his story, with a tone of resigned reluctance. "I wanted to wait because of my pack values, but before I met you, there was another girl I grew up with. Her father was a friend of my father, before he passed."

I knew little about his father's death, but his mother died at childbirth. That's why he had no other siblings.

"You know, I was a curious male, and when she told me she didn't want a mate, and decided she wanted to be with me, I went along with it, even though finding my mate was always my dream,' Rylan explained. That didn't irritate me as much as I thought it might. Instead, I felt a little bad for him.

195

"You must have been let down when you found out it was me who you were waiting for, all this time," I say solemnly. I feel him shake his head, as I veer away from that; he knows I regret the way I acted to some degree. "So, when I escaped for that year, you never were with anyone?"

Rylan makes a noise of distaste in his throat.

"Of course not. You were the only thing on my mind the entire time," he tells me. I feel suddenly better about myself.

"Well, since it's honest hour, I never thought of anyone else but you."

I could feel Rylan smile against my neck. He pulls me on top of him, to which I hardly protest at. Lying across his torso, I place my head on his chest so that I can listen to his heartbeat. He hasn't addressed what I just said, and I'm glad. Instead of talking, I feel my eyelids drift closed. I don't think I will ever be able to sleep without him ever again.

"I love you," I hear Rylan murmur, right before I fall asleep.

Perhaps I replied before sleep swept me away.

***

"She's very kind," Rylan tries to reassure me, motioning toward the door I should be walking through right now. It's the next morning, and honestly, I would rather be asleep right now, rather than confronting this problem....

I look at him flatly. "She's the moon goddess, you can't blame me for being a little nervous."

"She goes by Millicent, it's her given name, now," Rylan reminds me.

This is it. This is when I confront the moon goddess, or Millicent, rather, about the deal I shoved her into without talking to her about it first. Sinful seemed adamant that the deal goes through, especially on Millicent's side, which has me suspicious, but it's not my business to get myself into.

196

Instead, I plan to tell her what she needs to do, why, and the sacrifice that I had to make, along with Kace and Rylan, and then leave before she can get mad.

She may not have power right now ... but she's still considered a goddess.

"Seriously," Rylan says, nudging me softly. "There is nothing to be afraid of, she will take it in her stride, because that's what she's like."

Taking a deep breath, I have to open the door to the room, and hope he is right.

Because I'm about meet the third immortal in my life.

Chapter Thirty-Four

Dawn

If Rylan's hand wasn't against my back I wouldn't have stepped into the room.

I could see her the moment I looked up from my moving feet. She sat casually in the middle of the room, watching myself and Rylan as we enter. Her posture is painfully impeccable, her gaze sharp and direct. She's here for a reason ... to find out mine.

There are two chairs placed in front of her, ready for us to sit down on. Not looking at her for less than a second, I take a seat, Rylan taking his right beside me.

When I look up at her, I see ... a normal girl.

The mystical beauty that had once been explained to me isn't here. Her eyes have been shredded of every inch of soul that she might have previously possessed. The darkness of her hair either has always been like that, or wasn't, I'm not sure. She doesn't look right, and I know instantly why. This isn't the Moon goddess. This is Millicent, the one who had her powers taken from her. As per her request.

She doesn't say anything for a moment. Instead, she just watches. Taking that as a signal that she won't be talking until I do, I pose the first question.

"Why?" I breathe. "Why ask Fate to take your powers away, to suddenly want them back?"

I had to know. Rylan had explained the events to me, and how the alpha of independence summoned her from the Moon, to have Fate take her powers from her. Now, she wants her powers back, despite everything that she went through.

"I realized that my powers being taken affected more than just me. After news came back about Rylan's situation with his pack, I was devastated. I spent my entire life watching over the pack, listening to their songs and their prayers, knowing I would never be able to assist them ever again," she explains, her voice as light as air, running across my skin, raising hair on my arms.

"I was told you couldn't interfere," I say warily, again having the limits of her powers explained to me.

Millicent looks solemn, a slight frown creasing on her forehead. "I never did, that was why I wanted out. The suffering ... I could never watch it. I'm hoping I am able to have enough of Fate's power to do something by myself."

After hearing what happened the first time, I can't imagine what it's been like for her. She's over a million years old, and all of a sudden, she's a mortal, like me, regretting a decision she made. However, the way she speaks about Fate is strange, as if he's genuine and willing to give her any of his powers, despite the deal.

She seems to notice my doubtful expression.

"He tried to kill me once," she says, and I almost screw my face up. "What probably hasn't been explained to you or your mate, is that him and I were very much in love once. He pretends he doesn't remember, but he does. I knew he wouldn't kill me, and I know he will give me as much of his power as he pleases."

It's hard to believe Fate being in love with anybody. He seems heartless, soulless. How could someone like him ever please someone, especially the moon goddess?

"How bored were you up there?" I ask, not trying to sound so sardonic, but it happens naturally.

She smiles, despite herself. "He's another man when you reveal what's underneath, trust me. Now, we don't speak, although our

199

bond will always remain, even if that bond includes him threatening to take my life."

"Sounds complicated," I murmur. As I say this, I feel Rylan watching me. He's letting me speak, instead of interrupting, and now, he's watched me put Millicent's life into perspective. All of a sudden, having two mates doesn't seem so bad.

"Speaking of complicated, can I speak to you alone?" Millicent asks. She glances at Rylan, who nods.

With one last look at me, Rylan gently rubs my shoulder affectionately before he walks toward the door. I assume he knew this was going to happen, as he walks out with no reservations, happy to let us talk between each other. At least she's not Kace, who I have a feeling is about to be brought up in this conversation.

"I understand why you decided to strike that deal," Millicent says softly. "It was a very admirable thing for you to do."

That's the last way I thought she would describe my decision....

"You decided you would accept a new mate in order to save your mate's pack. Your pack too. It was a very big decision that only a luna could decide correctly, which makes me believe you will be a great one," she says warmly.

I'm not exactly sure how I should react to that. Clearly she wasn't the moon goddess when I was running from Rylan, fleeing from the entirety of the pack like it was a disease. When I think of a good luna for that pack, I think of anyone else over me. Millicent would do a much better job in my position.

"I wouldn't say it wasn't a difficult decision," I remind her uneasily. "I mean, I decided your fate for you, making you admit your love to your mate."

She slightly cringes at that reminder.

"You have two mates now, which I can't say will be very easy. I know Rylan, as the perfect alpha of purity and not as such. He hasn't taken this lightly, but he is very grateful for the sacrifice you have made. Many people are," she continues.

200

"Rylan hates this and it's not fair to Kace," I tell her, raking my hands back through my hair.

It's easy for Millicent to say how many people are grateful, considering she's not the one who has to live with the consequences. I'll never get to see these grateful people if Kace and Rylan make me lose my mind.

"Have you decided who will mark you on the night of the Ceremony?" she asks innocently, nearly making my heart stop. I've been so caught up in this deal, learning how to cope as a phantom wolf, and just with Ryland and Kace, that I haven't stopped to think about that. The idea has my head spinning, as I clutch the arms of the chair.

"Remember, Kace won't be involved in the ceremony, since he's not from the purity pack," Millicent says gently, watching my reaction carefully.

The idea of choosing either one of them nearly has me throwing up in front of the goddess, or former goddess. In my mind I always assumed it would be Rylan who I chose, but when I think about it some more, imagining the ceremony itself, I can't see who is there with me. It's as if my mind has decided I shouldn't be thinking about this.

Millicent looks grim.

"Don't push yourself hard to make the decision. The bond won't let you right now, especially not when you only just found out about Kace," she says, as if that's supposed to make me feel better.

"I think I need Rylan," I murmur breathlessly, ready to get up, but her hand on my knee stops me.

"You will only worry him, trust me," she says hurriedly.

She's right, as frustrating as that may seem. Slumping back in my chair, I curse whoever might be listening before I turn my attention back to Millicent. The expression on her face shows genuine sympathy, but that's not going to help, as nice as it may be.

"I'm sorry, I'm not the one who has to admit their love to their mate," I say, coming back to my senses as I relate my own situation to Millicent's.

In reality, I really want her to explain.

"Unfortunately, me admitting my love to my mate is not an easy feat for the either of us," she tells me softly, frowning slightly. She doesn't display many other emotions aside from happiness and sadness. That must be the effects of living for millions of years and seeing all there is to be seen.

I felt wary about asking her more on the subject, but I had to know. It will me kill not knowing why Fate and Sinful wanted her to do this so badly, and why they felt the need to take over Rylan's body to achieve it.

"Why are you so afraid?" I ask tentatively. "If you don't mind me asking."

"It won't be good for either of us, when I tell him," Millicent explains lightly. It's my turn to be the one to frown, as I struggle to see what she means by that.

"Why not?"

She exhales loudly, seeming to take an extra moment to think that through. "He and I are very different, if I'm honest. Once I tell him, things may change, if he wants them to. I've been quite happy keeping it from him."

"Does he know you're mates?"

She nods.

"Do you love him?"

She takes a moment to answer that question. I watch her as she stares off into space blankly, thinking about how she wants to answer that. I want to reassure her that I don't need an answer, however, she breaks me off.

"A lot."

I swallow. "Then what's the problem?"

"There are many problems. It's been millions of years since I last saw my mate, and if I'm honest, I've been running from him," she tells me, her eyebrow quirking up. My eyes widen at the familiarity of this. We are exactly same, even though her story is slightly more extreme. I suddenly feel a little less bad about what I did, knowing the moon goddess herself has felt the same way as me.

""Is he that bad?" I ask.

She chuckles softly. "I'm not really sure. But I love him, and for the better of my people, I will admit my love to him."

I had one more question that I needed to ask to be able to sleep tonight.

"So why were Fate and Sinful so obsessed with you doing this?" I ask her.

"Well," she says gently. "Sinful's my mate."

Chapter Thirty-Five

Dawn

"Seriously?" I splutter, not sure if I could really understand it. Who decided this? Who was the sick person that decided that Sinful and the goddess would be at all compatible together? I can tell by the look in Millicent's eyes that she doesn't want this at all, but the undeniable bond that even I once questioned has done its work, and she has no other choice but to fall for it.

She nods solemnly. "I've long since accepted it. Now, it seems, he wants more than that. He wants me to admit it."

"I'm so stupid," I mutter. "I would never have made that deal if I knew this."

"You don't have to worry. He can make me admit my love to him, but he can't make me want to be with him, which I assume is the end goal," Millicent says confidently. I have to admire her backbone, as I glance at Rylan, who was coming back into the room. He's not Sinful, I must remind myself. My mate actually has a heart.

Sinful's threats to my mate still loom in my mind.

"Do you know where he is?" I ask. "Sinful, I mean…"

Millicent pauses, her eyebrows creasing. I watch in silence as her eyes glaze over and she stares into space. The blank look is frightening, and for a moment, I'm convinced Sinful has taken over her body like he did with Rylan, until she speaks again.

"Sinful and I have a special bond that no other mates can replicate," she tells me, to which I furrow my brows at. "I know where he is at all the times."

Rylan and I exchange glances. "So where is he then?"

Millicent takes a deep breath, the blood running from her face. "He's here, in this pack, in this house."

For a moment, I lose all feeling in my limbs. That monster is here, in this house, with my sister, with Rylan? I suddenly feel violated, as if he's in the room with us, staring at me, ready to take everything that I love away from me. He isn't though, but by the look on Millicent's face, he has to be close.

"Where, exactly?" Rylan asks for me, sounding breathless.

All of a sudden, right in front of our faces, Millicent's eyes roll back, and she slumps forward. Rylan only just catches her before she falls head first into the ground.

"What ...What's happening?' I gasp, as Rylan pulls the unconscious girl into his arms.

Behind us, the door is flung open, the girl I met not so long ago running in. Milly, I think her name was. Her face is plagued by a face of utter worry. She looked so bad that I was convinced for a moment that she would throw up on the floor in front of us. She didn't even seem fazed at the sight of Millicent. Something else was on her mind....

"Dawn, you need to come right now," she insists breathlessly, holding her side. "It's your sister."

There was no need for an explanation. Millicent and Rylan were suddenly the last thing on my mind, as I scrambled out the room, desperate to see my sister. Did Sinful do something? If he did, I don't know how I would handle it. I would run away and never come back to this hell.

I find the chaos right in the middle of the house. Mara is on her knees, holding Lucy in her arms. I can't see my sister's face, as it's pressed against Mara, who sobs into the girl's hair.

At that moment, she looks so young ... so precious.

"What's going on?" I question, not sure if it's actually me talking.

There is no way Lucy is okay. Mara's face is streaked with tears, which it wouldn't be unless something had happened. Kaden

205

is nowhere to be seen, which is another red flag, since he's almost always at her side. But what really tipped me off, was how limp Lucy was. She was draped completely over Mara's lap.

"I'm ... I'm so sorry," Mara stutters, completely overcome with tears. I stand there, unsure what I should do. I'm numb.

"She's dead, isn't she?" I whisper, my voice dry as my throats feels stuffed with cotton wool.

Mara nods, and a part of me is instantly destroyed. A part no one would ever fill now. Not Rylan, not Kace, no one. There's no sadness though, not yet. Just anger, as my fists clench at my side, ready to kill whoever did this to an innocent young girl like Lucy. She's only ten years old ... I don't understand.

"I need to see her," I insist. I'm surprised I can't cry. I'm sure that will all come later. Right now, I just need to hold her.

Mara shakes her head. "You don't want to see her face."

At that moment, Lucy's head slightly shifts, and I could see the blood on Mara's shirt. Another flare of anger engulfs me to the point where I want to throw up. I'll mourn later. Right now, I need answers, and action.

"Who did this?" I snap, making Mara flinch.

"Kaden." She breathes. "Kaden did this."

I'm not sure how to react. For a moment, I expect Lucy to bring her head up and yell about how good she got me. But this is real. Mara isn't just torn by Lucy's death, but by who did this. Her mate ... the mate I'm about to try my best at killing.

"Where is he?" I ask, my tone softening. I have to hold onto this anger, otherwise I'll break down, and who knows what will happen then.

"He's gone. I kicked him out, and he's never coming near me, ever again," Mara vows, a fresh set of tears streaming down her face. "I don't want that monster anywhere near my daughter. Never."

The one thing I knew about Kaden and Mara, is that they loved each other. But now...

206

"Why would he do this?" I question. A while ago, I wouldn't have been surprised, but this time, I'm stunned. This isn't the Kaden I saw around Mara and Shaye, the good father. For him to turn around and kill an innocent ten year old girl just doesn't make sense. I didn't even get to talk to her about why she was so angry at Kace....

"She attacked Kace. Kaden was protecting him," Mara whispered. "He promised me he would control himself, that he would never kill again. I hate him."

I fall to my knees, my eyes on the poor girl in Mara's arms.

"She was only young ... I don't understand," I growl, trying to keep myself from punching something.

"He doesn't know his own strength, as a phantom wolf," Mara says, she furrows her brow, shaking her head. "Why am I defending him? He's a monster."

The door suddenly opens. Glancing over my shoulder, I expect to see Rylan, forgetting he was dealing with Millicent. Instead, I see Kace, and a new wave of absolute anger consumes me. I jump up, throwing myself at him. When I throw a fist at him, I expect nothing to happen, but when I hit his chest, he flies back, hitting the wall behind me.

He sinks to the floor, looking terrified of me. "Don't shift ... please don't shift."

Looking down at my hands, I try understand where this strength came from. Kace is much larger than me, and in one hit, I had him hitting the wall behind me as if I matched his height, or was even bigger.

Then I realized. I'm a phantom now. I may not have shifted, or shown any danger until now, which could explain the brewing strength and anger that I've been harboring.

"You don't deserve to live. Your brother killed my sister to protect you!"

I hardly realize I'm yelling. No, I'm screaming. I'm about to attack him again, to mess his face up like Kaden messed my sister up. I'm not going to ask how, but I'm sure it won't be as brutal as

207

what I'm about to give Kace. If only he was Kaden, who may be a phantom wolf, but he can't be as angry as I am now....

Before I can fully launch myself at my other mate, I feel hands on my arms, pulling me backward. There aren't any sparks, even when I expected Rylan.

The tie of anger between myself and Kace is snapped as I turn and shove my face into the chest of whoever is behind me. At this point, I don't care, as long as they aren't Kace or Kaden. Or Sinful.

"I'm so sorry...." I hear them mutter into my hair. "If only I knew this would happen."

Fate.

I would push away, but that would mean getting an inch closer to Kace.

Instead, Fate holds me back so he can properly look at me. When I first saw him, he was nothing but an arrogant prick who wanted nothing more than to strike a deal and win. Now, I see regret, and pain. He looks genuine, even if it's for just a second.

"Why are you here?" I snap, but I've lost all my fire. Now, it's laden with pain, the tears finally spilling to the surface.

"I'm taking you away from here."

I would have been worried in another circumstance, but now, I'm grateful that he is taking me away. There's only a simple shift of the breeze, and all of a sudden, I'm in another room, away from my sister. Away from Kace.

It's a doctor's room, I can tell. Millicent is on a bed, Rylan beside her. I suddenly don't care that she's ill.

All I care about is Rylan, as he turns and finally looks at me.

Chapter Thirty-Six

Dawn

"She's dead." I breath. "He killed her."

It took a moment for Rylan to register what I meant. While he blankly stared at me, I realized how badly my heart hurts. Lucy, my baby sister. I can't stand it.

"Oh Dawn, I'm so sorry," Rylan apologizes. I'm glad he isn't bringing anything else up, instead, letting me fall into his arms in grief. He could ask who did it, and why, but instead he only holds me, letting me finally cry.

I'm still numb. I know this is just an automatic reaction, that won't hit until later, when I notice her absence for real. Right now though, I have no idea how to handle this at all. Not until I can look Kaden in the eye and ask him why.

All of a sudden, a knock on the door draws me away from Rylan as I wipe my tears away. It's the doctor.

"We haven't found any clear reason as to why she wasn't woken," the doctor informs us solemnly. I grit my teeth. If Millicent doesn't wake up, this will never end. I'll never be able to escape the confines of the vengeance pack.

She lies right in front of us, dark hair sprawled out over her pillow. At first glance, she could almost seem dead, as she seems too peaceful, her hands folded neatly over her stomach.

I want to shake her awake, but I keep my hands to myself.

"We will wait with her, until she does wake," Rylan told the doctor, motioning at a seat beside the bed for me to sit on. The confidence in his voice was meant to reassure me that she will actually wake up, although I know she wouldn't. At least it seemed like she wouldn't. She seemed lost in another realm, one that she would never return from.

"This is such an inconvenience," I hear a sardonic voice say from the doorway.

Glancing over my shoulder, I meet the gaze of the last person I want to see right now. Okay, second to last. Kace.

He doesn't look at all fazed by what he sees in the room, or what happened out of it an hour ago. He looks untouched. I wish Lucy had killed him for whatever the reason she wanted to. Even if he wasn't the one to end her life …

"You have a lot of nerve coming in here," I growl under my breath, standing swiftly from my chair.

I hate how carefree he looks. When I look in his eyes, he doesn't reflect being the witness of death, or even the cause of it. He seems blank, and even slightly amused. It takes every ounce out of myself not to attack him, to finish what Lucy started. Plus, Rylan's hand on my arm is ready to hold me back, in case I were to commit to my thoughts.

"I've come to help, believe it or not," he says, which only flares my anger up more.

"Kace, I don't think you should be here right now. Dawn has been through ... a lot, and doesn't need anything else adding to it," Rylan reasons, the cool smoothness of his tone only helping sate my livid feelings slightly.

Kace sighs deeply, before he steps in anyway. The reasonable side of me is glad Rylan pulls my arm back, as I swipe so close to his face I could have done some serious damage.

Again, he doesn't seem fazed.

"I'm not here for you," he exclaims, "I'm here for Millicent."

Rylan doesn't say a word, so I follow in his suit, knowing it might be for the best. I'm glad the doctor left so he doesn't have to witness this as Kace takes a spot standing where he would have been. He blankly stares over Millicent, assessing her.

Then he brings his hand down to brush only her cheek, and with a gasp, the moon goddess is awake again, much to everyone's immediate shock.

"Yes, yes, it's so stunning, now would you leave?" Kace questions, seemingly bored with our presence. Millicent continues to gasp for air, as if she had been void of it, before she looks around, brightly alert.

"We aren't going anywhere," Rylan says carefully. How is he being so calm right now?

All I want is answers. As I watch Kace brush Millicent's hair back in an affectionate motion set for lovers only, I begin to realize that Kace might not really be Kace. A shudder of fear flutters down my body.

He seems to notice my expression. "Kace died a long time ago."

"What did you do with him?" I snap.

"Like I said, he died before you came close to meeting him. It's okay, you won't be seeing this body after I take Millicent away," he says calmly. I knew it was him. Sinful. Who else would take over someone's body without any remorse?

It makes me sick thinking about it. Was that Sinful the whole time? The moment I came back after witnessing Rylan having his body taken over by him, Kace was right there, waiting? It all makes sense. He's a mastermind; the devil. He doesn't care what he stands on to get his way, especially when it comes to his mate, Millicent.

"You aren't taking her anywhere," Rylan cuts in, although the doesn't sound so sure of himself. Easy for Sinful to catch on to.

"This is my mate, Rylan," Sinful says carefully. "Would you rather I take yours?"

Rylan's arms come around me protectively.

211

"That's what I thought," he says brightly. I'm surprised Millicent isn't protesting at all. She simply sits there, arm wrapped around Sinful's. Or Kace's. It's hard to makes sense of any of this right now. "But don't worry, I'm sending her back to the moon, where she belongs. She will have her powers back from Fate, and will once again look over your purity pack."

That seems too easy. Way too easy. Again, a mastermind at not only manipulating, but reading emotions, Sinful sees what I express.

"Your mate is smart, isn't she?" he says with amusement. "Of course, this comes at a price for someone else. Originally, the moon goddess gave up her powers for Fate's benefit. He used the excess power to turn an immortal into a mortal, who would work with him to manipulate people's fates. Her name is Destiny. Or was Destiny, at least."

I felt sick to my stomach.

"I took her speaking abilities away, to hinder her power, otherwise we would all surely be dead. Now, she has lost those powers, and is mortal. You now have the option to release Fate from my commands, and give Destiny her powers back before she dies of mortal old age," he says.

It is Rylan who speaks up for me. "We aren't making any deals."

"Oh please, this is no deal. This is simply an agreement, which, with one nod of Dawn's head, will be sealed," Sinful explains.

"Why would I want to help Destiny?" I question. "I don't even know her."

There is very little Sinful can manipulate me with. I don't trust him at all, which will never change, as long as I live. At this point, I've lost almost everything that I love, aside from Rylan, which means I'm not about to take anything from anyone. Especially someone who is considered all powerful.

"Well, if you agree, I can promise you certain things. Like maybe, your sister's life back," he says, raising his eyebrow in expectancy of my reaction.

212

Honestly, my heart almost stopped.

"Maybe I could even give Rylan a little bit of immortality, so you two can be together forever," he adds. I can feel Rylan tense behind me at the idea of that. It hasn't been on my mind so much at the moment, but it is definitely an issue we would have to face, otherwise I would be outliving him.

"What do you get out of this?" I question.

"Oh, this and that. It's all about the endgame. With Lucy, I'll be bringing someone else back, since I have a great leverage over Death. But you don't have to worry about them," Sinful continues.

Rylan moves up beside me, shaking his head. "We aren't agreeing to anything until you tell us your plan. Tell us why, Sinful, you are willing to bring her sister back."

"I have a few loose ties with some of the immortals here and there. No business of yours. I'm only using you for this as I have leverage. Just rest assured this makes all the difference," he tells us. Rylan is saying nothing again.

"Who will it hurt?" I question.

"No   one   you   know,"   Sinful   replies.

"Not me, not Rylan?"

"Of course not."

I exchange glances with my mate. Little of this makes sense, but I have a feeling anything Sinful says won't.

"You can't trust him," Rylan murmurs, shooting the immortal one of the dirtiest looks he could muster.

"I know that," I say carefully. "But this is Lucy. My sister who was murdered."

Sinful's smile is pure evil. "Pleasure doing business with you, Dawn."

Chapter Thirty-Seven

Two Weeks Later

Dawn

"She's your sister, Dawn, why are you so worried?"

I can't explain it. The idea of my sister being risen from the dead is daunting. Will she look the same? Will she get her body back? Nothing in my mind is coming together to make sense at all. Instead, it has me stressing out that the sister I knew won't be the same when Death brings her back.

Lucky for me, I won't have to meet Death. From what has been described of her, she doesn't seem like the ... nicest immortal to exist.

"It's so many things," I mutter, looking up at Rylan who crouches in front of where I sit, hands on my knees. He's been there for me all week. If I hadn't gotten Lucy back, I don't know what would have happened to me. I doubt I would be here, that's for sure.

"Everything will be fine. Once she is here, we will go back to the purity pack, life will be restored, and we can attend the mating ceremony," he says.

I know he is trying to be reassuring, but the cold, dark feeling in my stomach can't be so easily swayed by a few words in a promise. In addition to that, those exact words only make me feel worse;

trapped. I don't want to think about that right now, though. At this point, Lucy is the only matter I'm willing to deal with.

"When is Sinful getting here?" I question, trying to avert the conversation away from the ceremony. The more he goes on about it, the more likely I am to lose my mind.

Rylan bites the edge of his lip. "He won't be staying long. He will deliver your sister and leave promptly after. Then we won't have to deal with him ever again, trust me. This will all be over soon."

Before I can respond, a different expression flickers across his features. He glances over his shoulder, and suddenly, he's on his feet.

"I'll go down and check."

That sudden change in motive had my blood running cold. There is only one reason why Rylan would leave me like that out of nowhere. Only one person could manipulate something to happen in that way.

"It's a lovely day outside, isn't it?"

I grit my teeth as I turn around, seeing Fate leaning back against the bedroom window. Arrogant as ever. Nothing about him has changed an inch, even after the threat of his female counterpart losing her abilities. Either he isn't fazed by that at all, or he's putting on a facade just to deal with me. And I thought maybe him and I would have no reason to ever come face to face again. Guess I was wrong.

"And to what do I owe this pleasure?" I mutter, backing a few steps away from the bed. It gives the perfect amount of space for me to feel comfortable. "Was it completely necessary kicking Rylan out of the room?"

"He and I have already spoken about his duties as alpha. Now it's time for you and me to talk," he explains.

My fists clench at my sides. If he noticed, he didn't say anything.

"This is over, we both get what we want, now leave," I snap. In some ways I still can't summon an extreme amount of anger toward him, considering the deal to get my sister back would have never come about, had Destiny not existed. Still, he still had a cunning smile that I wanted to slap right off of him.

"Oh Dawn," he says coyly, "I'm here only to thank you. And to warn you."

"After you messed me around with Kace, I don't think any of your words will make a difference to anything I do."

It was Sinful's plan this entire time, I knew it. Fate simply was a chess piece in his little game, but I still somehow blamed him. Kace was killed a while ago, only for Sinful to take over his body when he pleased, keeping the entire idea of him alive. The thought of that made me sick to my stomach.

"I don't expect them to. I just want to firstly thank you for what you did for Destiny. I don't know what would have happened if her powers were taken forever," he admits honestly.

For the first time, I begin to see the semblance of an emotion there, that isn't related to his usual forthcoming self. He is truly grateful, which reminds of my situation with Lucy. I guess we both have to thank each other for something.

"Now a little warning about your sister," he says, his tone and expression taking on a more serious approach. My heart drops.

"What?" I ask warily.

"She attempted to kill Kace as she knew Sinful had control over his body. That girl was having premonitions that sparked the interest of many immortals, including him. I simply warn you that your sister may just be a little different by being brought back by Death - it turns the best evil - but she will be the topic of discussion of immortals everywhere until they find out how she did it. How she could tell," he exclaims.

I had to sit and let the information sit in my mind for a while. It confirmed my worst nightmare that Lucy wouldn't be the same once she is back.

216

"She's only young," I say carefully. "What would they do to her?"

He looks grim. "Unimaginable things, I would assume. Not all immortals are good. Some are more manipulative than me, have more secrets and won't stop until they uncover the secrets of others."

"What do you suggest I do then?' I question.

"You run, and you don't look back."

Fate strides forward a few steps, right past the bed to stand in front of me. He is a lot more intimidating up close, with those dark eyes hidden beneath mussed hair. I still stand here, waiting to make a move if it comes down to that.

"What about Rylan?" I ask softly. If Fate is who I think he is, he won't care about anything like that. All he will care about will be ... well, I'm not even sure anymore.

"You leave him, obviously. The purity pack is no place to hide your sister, and if he is not willing to protect her, then he is not worth your time. You should not feel obliged to be with your mate, there is always a choice. I suggest you don't go telling him that, though, unless you want to spend the rest of your life confined to a room."

The threat of his words are all too real, but leave Rylan? How could I do something like that to someone so fragile? The only reason I would ever do that is if it was because of my sister.

I won't lose her again.

"I'll get sick away from him. Eventually the both of us will die," I reason, making excuses up in my mind.

"Let him mark you then," Fate says simply. "Come on. I'm not telling you what you will do, I'm simply telling you what you should do. It's your choice, at the end of the day. Think of whose life is going to be sacrificed…"

Then he was gone. I can't tell if I blinked, or if he simply vanished into the air in front of me.

Sighing deeply, I fell back onto the bed. This all makes too much sense to have come from Fate's mouth. Leave Rylan and protect Lucy from immortals with the power of being a phantom wolf that I hardly know how to use? It seems so cruel. Yet so likely.

Digging my hands into my hair, I curse myself and the moon goddess, who should have resumed her position with the Moon once again.

Suddenly the door is thrust open, Lucy appearing on the other side.

She looks *exactly* the same. Her smile is so familiar that I'm instantly overcome with emotion. This is the same girl who left this world for only a moment. Death couldn't change something so beautiful. She can't ruin it, can she?

Rylan is behind her, as Lucy runs straight into my arms. The moment we touch I feel the bond of us being sisters slip right back into place.

"I hate myself for not protecting you," I murmur into her hair.

"Don't," is her only reply.

I'm refraining from asking all the questions I have right now. I'm curious to ask about her ability to sense that Sinful had taken over her body. I want to know what dying felt like. Most importantly, though, she clearly needs rest. It's as if I'm holding frail bones against my body, rather than my sister.

"Do you need anything?" I ask, finally separating myself from her. We both have to wipe our tears away.

"I'm a little hungry," she admits. It's such a simple request that I begin to cry again. It's hard to explain the feeling of seeing my sister alive. It's as if every worry in my life disappears, and everything makes sense again.

Rylan comes up to join us, wrapping his arm around my waist to comfort me.

"I'll take you down to the kitchen-"

She holds her hand up. "I'm fine. I just died, it's not the end of the world."

I watched in disbelief as she walks straight back out the door again. She has always been independent, which I admire her for.

"When's the mating ceremony?" I ask lightly, turning around to give Rylan my full attention.

His silvery blue eyes glisten. "Next week."

I smile softly, although my mind churns uneasily. I realize then, I have a decision to make.

Epilogue

Rylan

Dear Rylan,

I know this is hard to hear, after everything.

It's not as simple to explain as I thought it would be, when I picked up this pen to write to you.

I've always known that you were too good for me, and that you deserve better. I know you won't agree with me right now, but one day you will realize.

The decision was made when you marked me. I knew then.

I will leave and neither of us will get sick. Sadness is a given, but we can survive that, and move on.

I ask you please not to pursue us. Lucy and I can't be here, but you must. I can't explain it, I just have to ask you to trust me, and to understand that I don't belong here.

Someone once told me that no one should feel justified to stay with their mate.

You can hate me. I understand. What you don't understand just yet, is the reason why I have to do this. At the end of the day, it's to protect Lucy. And here I can't do that.

Thank you for trying. I'll miss you, my mate.

Dawn

I crush the note within my fist, having found it on my bedroom desk.